STACKS OF STORIES

Also available from Hodder Children's Books

Turning Points
The Forsaken Merman and Other Story Poems
Out of this World
Up to the Stars
Can I Buy a Slice of Sky?
Long, Tall, Short and Hairy Poems

Stacks of Stories

A Library Association Anthology

Edited by Mary Hoffman

Hodder
Children's
Books

a division of Hodder Headline Limited

To Hannah Kitty Vivienne Blake

*With thanks to all the contributors to this collection
who donated stories, artwork and time in support of
National Libraries Week.*

First published in Great Britain in 1997
by Hodder Children's Books
in collaboration with the Library Association

ISBN 0 340 69968 X

Typeset by Palimpsest Book Production Limited,
Polmont, Stirlingshire
Printed and bound in Great Britain by
Mackays of Chatham PLC, Chatham, Kent

Hodder Children's Books, a division of Hodder Headline Limited
338 Euston Road, London NW1 3BH

Contents

A Career In Witchcraft

Kaye Umansky

Illustrated by Doffy Weir

'Got anythin' on a career in witchcraft?'

Mr Smike gave a heavy sigh. He was in the middle of one of his favourite tasks – noting down the names of all the people who owed library fines. He could have done without the interruption.

He set down his pen with an irritable click and peered over the desk.

'What?' he said.

'I said, got anythin' on a career in witchcraft? Please?'

The speaker was a small girl, aged about sevenish, eightish, nineish, who cared? She stared solemnly

1

up at him through a pair of owlish glasses. She wore a black woolly dress and a cardboard witch hat decorated with clumsily cut out moons and stars. A plastic bin liner, pinned with safety pins, hung from her shoulders. She was clutching a small broomstick.

For a brief moment, Mr Smike was taken aback. Then, he remembered. Of course. Tonight was October the thirty first – Hallowe'en. The child was obviously all dressed up to go Trick Or Treating – an activity of which he heartily disapproved. Gangs of giggling vampires, skeletons, ghosts and masked monsters would be tramping the streets until all hours of the night, he supposed, leaning on doorbells and waving plastic bags under people's noses and demanding chocolate with menaces. Well, as far as Mr Smike was concerned, they could forget it. There would be no sweets, pennies or tangerines forthcoming from *him*. Any child unwise enough to come calling at *his* house tonight would get nothing but a stiff lecture.

'Careers over in the corner,' said Mr Smike, shortly.

'Which corner? There's four,' said the small girl.

'That one.' He jerked his head. 'And you can leave that stick here,' he ordered severely. 'I don't want bits of twig scattered all over the floor.'

For a split second, the small girl looked mutinous. Then, she gave a little nod and carefully propped her broomstick against the desk before heading off between the book racks. Mr Smike watched her, noting with disapproval that her socks had fallen down.

Mr Smike wasn't fond of children. Noisy, ill-mannered little brats with their shrill little voices and grubby little hands. The less he had to do with them, the better. Normally he would be over in the reference section of the main library, but Mrs Jaunty, the children's librarian, had rung in sick and there was nobody else to fill in.

He cast a jaundiced eye over the place. Picture books, hah! Cushions, jigsaw puzzles, mobiles, posters, murals, double hah! This wasn't a proper library. It didn't have QUIET notices all over the place. There wasn't even a box marked FINES. Great hordes of school children had been in and out all day, putting their unwashed fingers all over the books. The place had been chock-a-block with chattering mums pushing buggies full of snotty-nosed toddlers who waddled around the place getting underfoot. They treated the place like a hotel. It wasn't his kind of library at all.

Oh well. Thankfully, it was nearly closing time. With a bit of luck, that Jaunty creature would be back tomorrow, dispensing books and smiles and organising poetry competitions and story telling sessions and whatever else the silly woman did to keep the little monsters happy.

Mr Smike picked up his pen and returned to his list. Mrs C. Randall – two books, three weeks overdue at twenty pence a day, that would be eight pounds forty. Wayne Geeke, four books out on motorbike maintenance, should have been returned a month ago, that would be twenty two pounds forty and serve the cocky young lout right for having such an anti-social hobby. Old Albert Bedlam, the large print version of *Managing On A Low Income*, a full ten days overdue. Two pounds exactly. That'd make a tidy hole in his pension. J. Sugden, six books out, two weeks late, oh, excellent, excellent! Now let's see, that would be . . .

'There isn't one.'

The small girl was back again, ogling him over

the desk with her magnified eyes which were, he noticed, a kind of fishy green.

'Isn't what?' snapped Mr Smike.

'A *Career In Witchcraft* book. There's nursin' and hairdressin' an' ballet dancin' an' lawyerin' an' bein' a TV presenter an' that, but nothin' on witchcraft.'

'In that case,' said Mr Smike, with great satisfaction, 'I can't help you, can I?'

There was a little pause. Mr Smike went back to his list, hoping that the annoying child would give up and go away.

'Where's the lady?' asked the small girl, standing her ground.

'At home, sick,' Mr Smike told her, with even greater satisfaction.

'The lady'd help me. She's nice. She found me lots of useful stuff. Spells and that. That's how I got my broomstick goin'. Couldn't get it to budge until she helped me find the right book. Goes like the clappers now.'

She reached out and gave the propped up broomstick a satisfied little pat.

'Indeed,' muttered Mr Smike, not looking up.

'Oh, yes. She got me a great book on *Herbs What*

Can Heal. I can get rid of warts now. And boils. You got any warts or boils need fixin'?'

'No.' Mr Smike glanced pointedly at the library clock. Only another two minutes, then he could throw out this revolting child and never again have to endure her bizarre fantasies.

'Got anythin' new in on toads?' persisted his tormentor.

'No.'

'Bats?'

'No.'

'Anythin' that'll tell me where to get hold of an eye of a newt?'

'Little girl.' Mr Smike spoke wearily. He leaned forward and frowned down at her, tapping his pen. 'Little girl. Don't you think this obsession with witchcraft is a little unhealthy? What does your mother say?'

'Oh, she's all for it.' The small girl placed her elbows on the desk in what Mr Smike considered to be an over-familiar way. 'Well, she would be, wouldn't she? Bein' one herself an' that.'

'I beg your pardon?'

'Ma. She's a witch.'

'Oh, I *see*! And I suppose she's back in the cave, mixing up a brew?' enquired Mr Smike with cold sarcasm.

'Well, it's not a cave,' the small girl informed him seriously. 'This isn't the dark ages, you know. It's a proper house. But you're right about the brew. She's getting it ready for tonight's party. All me aunties are round helpin', an' cacklin' so loud I can't do me homework. Ma said to come along here an' look up stuff for meself in the library. She's trainin' me up, but she reckons you learn better if you look up stuff for yourself. An' that's what I'm doin'.'

'It's a great pity she hasn't trained you up not to tell lies, young lady,' said Mr Smike nastily. 'There are no such things as witches.' He pointed to the clock. 'See that? One minute to closing time. I suggest you remove your elbows from my desk, choose yourself a suitable book and then run along home.'

'I don't tell lies,' objected the small girl. Her green eyes flashed. 'An' there *are* such things as witches!' she added, with spirit. 'I know, 'cos I'm gonna be one. So there.'

'One minute,' repeated Mr Smike through gritted teeth.

The small girl stared at him.

'You don't believe me, do you?' she said.

'I most certainly do not believe you,' replied Mr

Smike grimly. 'I've never *heard* such twaddle. Too much television, that's your trouble.'

'We haven't got a television. Ma's got a crystal ball, but I'm not allowed to use it. Except on Saturday mornin's when she's havin' a lie in.'

Mr Smike had had enough of all this. He wagged a warning finger under the small girl's nose.

'Young lady,' he said. His voice was so sharp, you could have sliced cucumber with it. 'This is not funny. You can take a joke too far. Some people may find your flights of fancy amusing, but I am not one of them.'

There was a short silence. The small girl continued to stare at him. The clock ticked. Then:

'So you don't have anythin' on a career in witchcraft, then?'

'No!' shouted Mr Smike. 'I do not! You have no business wandering in here pestering busy adults with your ridiculous requests. You are a silly little girl with a head full of rubbish. And you can tell your mother I said so.'

The small girl went very red. There was another short silence. Then:

'I could turn you into a frog, I could,' she

muttered with a scowl. And she turned abruptly on her heel and set off back down the racks.

Mr Smike felt pleased with himself. He had told her, oh yes indeed. You had to be firm with these cheeky young things. Briskly, he gathered up his papers, slipped them into his briefcase and clipped his pen into his breast pocket. He would finish the list at home. It would be something to look forward to after supper. Then, if there was time, he would write another of his complaining letters to the local paper. (Mr Smike wrote a lot of complaining letters to newspapers. It was a kind of hobby. He wrote about the state of the drains, the surliness of dustmen, the laziness of the unemployed and the trouble with Youth Today. If the paper didn't publish them, he wrote and complained about *that*.)

He opened a drawer, took out the library key in readiness and waited, eyes on the clock, tapping his foot impatiently and willing it to move on. Thirty seconds to go.

'I'll take this one,' said the small girl, appearing again and slamming a book under his nose. '*Baba Yaga*. It's got my great, great, great, great,

great-gran in it. She was Russian, you know,' she added, with a certain amount of defiant pride.

'Ticket,' said Mr Smike coldly, snapping his fingers.

The small girl rummaged beneath her bin liner and slid a ticket across the desk. Mr Smike inspected it. *Agnethia Toadfax. 13, Coldwinter Street.*

Ridiculous name for a child. But then again, the child was ridiculous, with her tacky home-made costume and overheated imagination.

To his intense disappointment, the ticket seemed to be in order. In stony silence, he stamped the book and pushed it across.

'Right,' he said curtly, pointing to the door. 'No more of your nonsense. Out.'

Agnethia Toadfax opened her mouth, seemed to be about to say something, then closed it again. She picked up her broomstick, tucked her book under her arm and marched out the door without another word.

Mr Smike shook his head and tutted for a considerable length of time. Whatever were parents coming to these days? A good, sharp smack or two, a sight less television and a daily dose of something nasty in a spoon, that's what was needed. With a sniff, he rose, collected his coat and went to turn out the lights.

Outside, high above the library roof in the cold October night, Agnethia Toadfax hovered on her broomstick. Her hair streamed out and her bin-liner cloak flapped madly in the leaf-spinning wind. Below her, the street lamps spilled pools of orange light into the dark, empty street. Up above, wild clouds raced across the full moon.

Should she or shouldn't she? Ma had told her to be careful, to use The Power wisely and not let her temper get the better of her – but then again, everyone was entitled to a little fun. Especially someone who was just setting out on a Career In Witchcraft. And it *was* Hallowe'en . . .

'Ah, to heck with it,' she muttered, and twiddled her fingers in a Certain Way. Then, stifling a little giggle, she wheeled her broomstick and headed for home.

It went like the clappers.

Behind her and far below, Mr Smike was strug-gling to turn the key in the lock of the library door.

It was proving a difficult task. Particularly with the thin green webs which had suddenly sprouted between his fingers . . .

Knocking the Head off an Alien

Jacqueline Wilson

Illustrated by Nick Sharratt

I came home from school to find a two metre tall rabbit staring at itself in my Mum's wardrobe mirror. It gave a little squeal when it spotted me. I gave a little squeal too, though I'm not usually a squeally sort of person.

'Oh Noel, you gave me a fright creeping up on me like that!' said the rabbit, trying to pull its head off.

I'm Noel. Like 'The first Noel the angel did say . . .' It's what everyone sings when I tell them my name. The first thing they *say* is 'I bet you were born on Christmas Day, right?' Wrong! I was born in July. (My birthday was actually in five days time and I was looking forward to it like anything.)

Mum called me Noel after her favourite writer when she was a little girl. That's typical of Mum. She's a librarian. I know exactly what name I'd have been saddled with if I'd been a boy. *Roald*.

'Oh no. It's stuck!' said the rabbit, tugging and twisting its head.

'Come here,' I said, sighing. I reached up and got hold of both ears.

'Careful! Don't pull them off!' said the rabbit.

One quick flick and I had the huge furry head in my arms. My mother's own face, very pink and damp, blinked at me from the top of the giant rabbit get-up.

'Honestly, Mum! You don't half look a twit,' I said.

'I know,' said Mum, trying to wriggle out of the rest of it.

'You're not going to appear in *public* like that?' I said.

Mum nodded.

'Maria said she'd do the rabbit story-telling session, but now both her twins have gone down with chicken-pox so she can't possibly come to the Summer Fun Day.'

'So when *is* this super fun event?' I said, helping Mum skin herself.

Mum looked at me anxiously.

'*Mum*?'

'Well – it's this Saturday, Noel.'

'But that's my *birthday*! We're going to the Flowerfields Shopping Centre. And we're having lunch at McDonald's. And then we're going to a film. You *promised*!'

'I know,' said Mum. 'And we'll still do it all – *after* the library fun day. Oh Noel, I'm sorry.' Mum paused, one leg still trapped in rabbitskin. 'Please say you don't mind too much.'

'I mind *heaps*,' I said. 'Look, you go and tweak your ears and waggle your powder-puff tail. I'll stay at home and watch telly till you're through.'

'You can't stay at home by yourself without anyone to look after you,' said Mum. 'Oh, *blow* this silly costume.' She gave the leg a last tug, toppled, and fell thump on her bottom.

'You're the one who needs looking after,' I said, unhooking her leg and picking her up. 'Okay, okay, I'll go. Just don't expect *me* to have fun, okay?'

Mum woke me early on Saturday with a little pile of presents. I felt them all first.

'Don't worry, there isn't a single book,' said Mum.

She's given up on me with books. When I was little we had story sessions all day long and it was like I was permanently caged in a zoo with Little Bear and The Very Hungry Caterpillar and The Tiger who came to Tea and Frances the Badger and Elmer the Elephant and all the Wild Things. It was okay, I suppose – but then I got big enough to read to myself and somehow I couldn't be bothered. I'd always much sooner watch telly or play on a computer. Mum tried s-o-o-o-o hard to find me the right book that would spark off the reading habit. Now she pretends she doesn't mind a bit. Ha!

She gave me two videos for my birthday. 'Little Women' and 'A Little Princess'.

I tried to look enthusiastic. (Maybe I could whip them back to the shop and swop them for some wondrously gory horror movies?).

The last present was *much* better – a pair of Nike trainers. Mostly I have to make do with Woolies cheapies so this was seriously special.

'You are a Mega-great mother,' I said, giving her a hug.

I had cards and stuff from The Body Shop and music tokens and chocolates and a game and some felt tips from my friends. Nothing at all from my father.

'Don't say he's forgotten again,' Mum said wearily. 'I'll phone him up. It's too bad of him.'

'No, it's great, because he'll feel so guilty when you tell him he'll probably send me a whacking great cheque,' I said.

I can act really cool about my parents splitting up. Well, nowadays. We're fine, Mum and me. Just so long as she doesn't muck things up with a boyfriend. There's this Total Drip who works at the library and fusses round her.

He was fussing in overdrive when mum and I arrived at the park where the Fun Day was being held, setting up all the stalls and dashing around being drippily keen and enthusiastic. I assumed his amazingly nerdy woolly cap was his own personal choice of headgear – but Mum told me he was being Wally.

'Yes, he's a right wally if you ask me,' I said.

Mum gave me a nudge.

'He's being *the* Wally. You know, in the *Where's Wally* books? He's going to hide among the crowds and give every child a lollipop if they can spot him,' said Mum.

I felt Mum was being a bit optimistic. The crowds were rather thin on the ground so far. While she struggled into her rabbit costume in the Library Van I wandered round the stalls, yawning. There were Book Quizzes galore, a Face Painting stall, a *Charlie and the Chocolate Factory* sweet stall, a Fairy Tale Bouncy Castle, an author's signing table, all the usual stuff. Plus there was a strange sort of coconut shy, only there weren't any coconuts, just painted green heads set up on sticks.

'Knock the head off an Alcazar Alien,' said Jenny, one of my Mum's mates at the library.

'Knock the head off a *what*?' I said.

'*You* know, Noel. Haven't you read the Alcazar Science Fantasy series? You'd love them. They're very popular with kids who . . . who don't like reading very much.' She lowered her voice as she said the last bit, as if it was a serious social disease.

I laughed.

'No thanks,' I said. 'But I'll have a go at knocking the head off one of the Ally Alien thingies.'

It wasn't as easy as I'd thought. I'm usually absolutely ace at coconut shies, but these little green alien heads were jammed so firmly on to their stands one didn't even wobble when I hit it first go. I don't like to admit defeat. So I had another go and another and another. Jenny said I didn't have to pay as my Mum was staff. Besides, I was good at drumming up custom.

There were quite a lot of people in the park now. No-one seemed particularly interested in spotting the sad substitute Wally – and sadly not a lot of kids were surrounding the Rabbit in the story-time corner. But there were heaps gathering round the alien shy – and it was a good job *I'm* not shy because most of them were watching me. I was getting the knack of it now. I worked out how to get enough spin on the ball to catch the alien head *whack*, just where its temple would be – and it shot up and keeled off its stand with a satisfying *kerplonk*. All the kids cheered.

I queued up again but didn't get so lucky the next time. There were masses and masses of people in the park now, mostly clustered round this stall. The next time I felled *two* alien heads with just three balls.

'Wow! You've definitely hit the jackpot, Noel. Here's your prize,' said Jenny.

I was pretty chuffed – until I saw what the prize was. A paperback omnibus of Alcazar Alien stories.

'Oh yuck!' I said.

'Yuck?' said this guy standing nearby, with this great cluster of kids all round him.

I wondered if he was their school teacher or something, though he didn't *look* a bit teachery in his black shirt and black jeans. He looked pretty fit. Maybe he was some celebrity footballer (with a new book of football tips?) Mum's colleagues had somehow duped into attending their Fun day? But then I'd surely recognise him? He looked so cool, with his tousled blonde hair and dark brown eyes. No, cancel the footballer idea, this guy could well be a rock star (here to publicise his book of greatest hits?). Yes, because lots of the kids had autograph books.

'I take it you don't go a bundle on the Alcazar Omnibus?' this guy said to me.

Jenny was blushing and mouthing stuff at me. I felt a bit embarrassed. I didn't want to come across as this really rude ungrateful bratty kid (though *three* wins ought to have a Mega-great Triple Whammy Prize – not just a boring old book).

'Well, I haven't ever read this stuff,' I said.

'You'll *love* the Alcazar stories, you really will,' said Jenny, bright-red in the face.

I didn't see why she was making such a big thing of it.

'You know I'm not really into books,' I said. 'I find reading pretty boring, actually.'

'Noel!' Jenny squeaked, in seeming agony.

'Don't you know who he is?' said one of the kids, sniggering at me. 'He's Peter Foster.'

It didn't connect at first. Peter Foster, footballer, rock star . . . ? Then I saw a name in big silver letters on the Alcazar book. Peter Foster, *author*!

'Oh gosh,' I said, going hot all over.

But it was okay. He didn't look a bit offended. He was laughing.

'I find *writing* pretty boring a lot of the time,' he said. 'Don't worry, Noel. I don't mind a bit if you don't read my book. I'm sure you've got heaps of more interesting things to do. You're obviously a girl of action. You've certainly got a really lethal way of bowling. I think we'd *all* better watch our heads!'

I shuffled my feet in my new Nike trainers, thrilled that he was being so cool.

'Maybe I'll give the book a go after all, seeing as it's by you,' I said. 'Would you sign it for me?'

So he wrote: 'To Noel, who is *not* my number one fan! I promise you don't have to read this book. Yours, Peter Foster' and he did a little picture of himself too, a tiny stylish pinman all in black, waving at me.

I showed it to Mum. She squinted through her rabbit eyes and said, 'Oh, isn't that lovely of him. But I hope you weren't too cheeky.'

'I didn't *mean* to be cheeky. I just didn't twig who he was at first.' I was flicking through the first few pages. It didn't look *too* difficult. There were lots of talky bits – and he didn't seem to take this space stuff too seriously. I read one really funny paragraph and giggled.

I looked up. The rabbit was peering at me.

'Okay, okay,' I said. 'I'll give it a try.'

'Good,' said Mum.

She tried to sound *ever* so casual. Her rabbit head stayed immobile. But I could tell she was practically clapping her bunny paws together in glee.

I read the entire omnibus over the weekend (and

there wasn't much of Saturday left after we'd finished at the Fun day and had our Big Macs and French Fries and pottered round the Flowerfields Shopping Centre *and* been to a film – a truly scary creepy horror movie. Mum ended up hiding her head in my lap!).

Dad sent a cheque the next week. A big one, just as I'd predicted! I bought myself a new football strip – and several Peter Foster paperbacks. (I looked in the library too, but they were in such demand I could never find them on the shelves.)

I read them in a great happy rush. Old Jenny was *right* for once. Then I phoned her up and wheedled Peter Foster's address from her.

I wrote him this letter, telling him I'd read his book after all, *lots* of his books, and guess what – maybe I *was* his number one fan after all!

Hugs and Kisses

Adèle Geras

Illustrated by Jan Ormerod

I did it. OK, I didn't do *all* of it, but I was the one who pointed the way at exactly the right moment, so I'm taking some of the credit. My brother is different. He's been changed forever, and he's changed for the better. I didn't object to the way he was before, but I'm his sister, so I'm biased. Still, just because I adore him doesn't make me blind. I could see – I've always been able to see – that in most people's eyes he was, if not exactly a nerd, then certainly a very long way away from being cool. Would you like a bit of a description of him? His name is Hugh. I call him Huge because he's quite slim and small. He's sixteen, with brown, floppy hair and brown (I nearly said 'floppy') eyes. I realize this doesn't tell you very much, and believe me, I've done my best for ages to turn him into something resembling Tom Cruise. That would make life easier. I could just say: 'Picture Tom Cruise' and you'd know what to imagine. I've made massive efforts to get him to dress properly, in fashionable clothes that would do what the magazines always say clothes are supposed to do for you – you know, make a statement – but all my struggles are in vain. Whatever he buys, he always magically ends up wearing:

- T-shirt and jeans in summer
- Sweat-shirt and jeans in normal winter
- Sweater and jeans in totally icy weather.

I'm not talking designer things, either. Ordinary, boring everything, and whatever colour they're meant to be, they always give an impression of Black.

'I don't want to look as though I'm trying too

hard,' is what he says when I yell at him. 'I thought girls hated that.'

'That's trying too hard,' I sigh. 'You don't try at all.'

'Never mind,' he says. 'At least I'm clean.'

That's true. The fact that Hugh showers and shampoos his hair every single day is one of my greatest successes. It's all down to me.

'BO,' I told him two years ago 'is Turnoffsville, Arizona. No girl will come within feet of you. You *have* to shower every day.'

'The way you express yourself,' he said, 'leaves something to be desired. Turnoffsville, Arizona indeed! Wherever do you find such expressions?' Hugh gave one of his armpits a sniff and winced. 'Still, I see what you mean. I'll give showering a go, then.'

He's been as good as his word. Now he's sweet-smelling all right, but it hasn't helped. He hasn't, as far as I know, been within feet of a girl. And it wasn't because he didn't want to, because he did.

'All boys are dying to go out with someone,' I told my friend Mandy. 'It's just that a lot of them don't know how to make the first move.'

I'd decided that, left to himself, Hugh would no

more approach a girl than rob a bank, and that I had to do something.

'All boys,' said Mandy, 'except the ones who want to go out with other boys. Maybe Hugh is gay.'

'He isn't,' I told her. 'He's just emotionally illiterate. I read about that in a magazine. It means you feel all the right stuff you're supposed to feel, only you can't find the words to tell anyone about it.'

'What did he say?' Mandy wanted to know, 'when you said that?'

'He snorted, and said I'd got no room to talk because I was computer-illiterate.'

'Are you?'

'I suppose I am, but I can't say I'm that bothered about it. I'm more interested in human hearts than in machines. I tell him you can't cuddle a machine.'

'What does Hugh say to that?' Mandy asked.

'He explains very patiently that there's more to life than cuddling, but I think he's only saying that to cheer himself up. All his friends have got girlfriends. They're beginning to tease him. He's spending more and more time in front of his computer. I despair.'

This conversation, of course, was Before. We are now in the land of After. Hugh is transformed, and this is how it happened. I'm thinking of writing a guide book for other sisters, and my first and most important chapter will be called: 'Where to find Romance.' It will be a very short chapter, consisting of three words: 'The Public Library'. There. I bet you're surprised. I bet you've never in a million years thought of a library as being Romantic. Well, it is. And what's more (this is very important if you're young and haven't got any money), it's FREE.

But I'd better get back to the beginning of the story. Please imagine a snowy day in the Christmas holidays. Hugh got it into his head that he had to work. He had to do this even though the sun was shining, and even though I'd pointed out to him that the park was probably full of Supermodel Lookalikes, just waiting for a Chance Encounter. I'm a great believer in Chance Encounters. I mapped it all out for Hugh. A snowball could get thrown, an SL would get hit, and then the conversation would go something like this:

Hugh: 'Gosh, I'm so sorry. I really wasn't trying to hit you.'

SL: 'That's OK.' (Batting eyelashes) 'I was just wishing I had someone to play snowballs with.'

Hugh: 'My name's Hugh. What's yours?'

SL: 'Cindy.' (or Claudia, or Kate or whatever.)

Hugh: 'Gosh, Cindy,' (or whatever) 'I don't think I've ever seen eyes so brown.' (Or green, or blue . . . delete whichever does not apply.)

This scene was supposed to end with Hugh and SL walking off towards the duckpond together, holding hands. I described it brilliantly, but Hugh was very scathing.

'You,' he said, 'have seen too many deodorant ads.'

'You,' I said, 'have no imagination and a heart of stone.'

'I've got more imagination than you, sister dear.' He grinned. 'You seem to have vanished completely out of this scenario. What have you done with yourself? Mum'd kill me if I took you to the park and just left you on a bench somewhere while I mooched off into the sunset with an SL.'

I sniffed at him. '*If* it were to happen, I'd just

32

melt tactfully away, and leave you alone with your beloved.'

'And *I'd* still get into trouble. You're not allowed to melt away when you're with me, as you know very well.'

So there we were. Hugh wanted to work, and what's more he'd got it into his head that he needed to go to the library in order to do it. This wouldn't have affected me normally, but on this occasion, Mum was going to be out all day, and if there was one Iron Law in our house, it was this: 'Lydia is not to be left at home on her own on any account. If there's no-one to babysit, then anywhere Hugh goes, she goes too.'

I resent this. I resent it bitterly, and moan about it every chance I get. For all I know, Hugh moans about it too, but he must do it inwardly, because I've never heard him complain. I say: I'm eleven. I'm grown-up. I'm responsible. I used to be Milk Monitor. I collect money for Sick Animals. I'm a GOOD GIRL. None of this helps. My Mum looks enigmatic and mutters about the World being wicked, however good I might be, and she also mutters about the Law. Apparently, eleven-year-olds are not legally supposed to be left all alone.

I must find out one day if this is true. Perhaps I could look it up at the Library. I wouldn't put it past my mother to have made it up, just to keep me in my place.

So there I was, setting off with Hugh for the library. Please don't get me wrong. I like the library as much as the next person. I like books and I like reading and I've been going to our branch since I was a tiny tot. They used to have cutting and pasting sessions every Wednesday afternoon, and Miss Thompson used to read us lovely stories while we made collages from old magazines. I wouldn't be without my library for anything, but I definitely used to think of it as a place to go into and out of, rather than somewhere one would choose to spend hours and hours of a day in, especially a day during the holidays.

'Find yourself a good book,' Hugh said as we went in, 'and go and read it on one of the comfy chairs. I'll be over in the Architecture section.'

'What's this work, then?' I asked, just to be friendly.

'I'm designing a city,' he said. 'It's an I.T. project for school. You can come and give me a hand looking things up, if you like.'

'Maybe later,' I said. 'I'm going to go and find something to read first.'

'OK,' said Hugh, but his mind, I could tell, was full of computer-generated skyscrapers and walkways. 'See you.'

I found a book almost at once. It was called *The Curse of the Bloodsucker* and I hoped Hugh was going to be in the library for ages, because it looked brilliant, and I wasn't sure Miss Thompson or her assistants would let me take it out. They operated their own personal method of censorship in this branch. Certain books weren't exactly forbidden to juniors, but Miss Thompson used to come over all auntieish and say:

'Oh, goodness me, dear, you wouldn't really like that, you know . . . it's very cheap, thin stuff and not in the least frightening. But I have got a complete Edgar Allan Poe and he really *did* write scary stories.' Then out would come a volume with thousands of pages and tiny print and I'd be expected to abandon my lovely little paperback with the shiny bloodstains and glittering knives all over the cover.

I took *The Curse* . . . over to the armchairs and

settled down. There was a machine in the corner which people used to help them look at old newspapers. I'd had a go on it once. The newspaper was photographed on to a roll of film and you slotted the roll in and turned a handle and there was the bit you wanted to read ready for you on a lit-up screen. A young woman was sitting at the machine and she was doing so much sighing and fidgeting and moaning that I couldn't concentrate. I looked at her, wondering whether I dared ask her to stop making such a racket. She was wearing jeans and a black sweatshirt and had long, floppy brown hair hanging down in such a way that I couldn't see her face properly. I said: 'Excuse me' and she turned towards me.

The words I was planning to say next never got said. This person was really pretty. She had soft brown eyes with long eyelashes, and, although she'd obviously never heard of make-up, her complexion was gorgeous. She had the sort of skin you wanted to touch, just to see if it felt as good as it looked. I liked her at once. She reminded me of someone, and it took me about a second and a half to realize that she was practically Hugh's twin. She looked much more like him than I did.

If I'd been in a cartoon, this would have been the moment when a lightbulb lit up above my head. I said quickly:

'I'm sorry to disturb you, but I can see that you're having a bit of trouble with that machine, aren't you?'

'Oh, I am,' she said. 'I'm useless. I can never get it to work. Are you good with stuff like this?'

'No,' I said and tried to look dead casual as I went on, 'but my brother's brilliant and he's just over there in Architecture. I'll go and get him.'

'But,' she started to say. It was too late, though. I was running through Fiction before the word was out of her mouth.

'Huge,' I whispered and could hardly catch my breath, what with combined excitement and rushing. 'Could you come over to that newspaper-reading thingie?'

'Microfiche,' said Hugh. He always knew the right name for everything.

'Whatever,' I said. 'There's someone there who doesn't know how it works, so I said you'd help.'

Hugh sighed. 'OK, I suppose so, but I do wish you wouldn't do your Little Miss Helpful act when I'm busy.'

'It won't take a second,' I said. 'Truly.' I was patting myself on the back because I hadn't mentioned that the person in need of help was a girl.

'It'd better not,' he said. 'I was getting on dead well.'

When Hugh caught sight of her (I didn't have a name for her at that point), I saw him stop and half-turn to walk away, but I was right beside him, and I wasn't going to let this opportunity slip past. I grabbed his hand and dragged him towards the micro-thingie machine saying in a voice louder than the one I usually use in the library:

'Here he is. This is my brother, Hugh.'

The girl got up from her chair.

'Thanks so much for coming to help me,' she said. 'I really never meant to disturb anyone. I'm ever so sorry.'

Then it happened. It really did. In Real Life. I'd only ever seen it in the movies before, or on TV, but it happened right in front of me, and it was true. She looked at him, and blinked, and kept looking at him. He looked at her, and I could feel him trembling because for some stupid reason, I was still holding his hand. I let go of it at once. Hugh coughed. Then he pushed his hair back. They just kept on staring at one another. Then she said: 'My name's Chrissie,' which was quite a long sentence, considering Hugh only managed one syllable in return.

'Hugh,' he said, and I wondered if I should say something, but I looked at Chrissie and I could see that she knew exactly what she was doing. I've talked to her about it, now that she's Hugh's girlfriend, and she says:

'Once I'd seen him, he'd had it. I wasn't going to let him get away.'

The strange thing is that, in spite of never having had a girlfriend before, Hugh took to being in love like a duck to water. If he could read this, he would say: 'What a cliché!' but I don't care. Clichés only got to be clichés because they're so true. Hugh and Chrissie *did* remind me of two ducks, swimming around happily on a pond, beaks touching, and feathers (clothes!) matching. They spend a lot of time together in the library.

'It's warm,' says Hugh, 'and there are so many things to look at, and best of all, Mum is far away, and not asking me questions about Chrissie's family history.'

I don't have to ask if he loves her. I know he does. I proved it the other night. Chrissie rang up and asked to speak to 'Hugs'. It took me a moment to realize who she meant.

'Hugs?' I said.

'I mean Hugh.' I could feel her blushing over the phone.

'I'll get him,' I said, and called up the stairs.

'Huge,' I shouted. 'It's for you.'

'Who is it?' he said.

'It's Chrissie.'

He came bounding down the stairs and grabbed the phone.

'Kisses,' he breathed. I couldn't believe my ears. She called him Hugs, and he called her Kisses . . . well, I suppose it's not that far removed from Chrissie, for someone who's taken leave of their senses. Obviously neither of them cared that they sounded like a pair of wallies. I couldn't *wait* to tell Mandy.

A Picture of Home

Bernard Ashley

Illustrated by Caroline Binch

Ugaso Samatar looked round the big classroom. It had more than thirty children in it; but there were no other Somali children, no-one else who spoke her language.

'Aabe!' It was real scary, being in Britain. Not scary like running away from the stench of burning villages or the sound of shooting. And not scary like trying to get behind a stunted thorn-bush, hiding from the rival clansmen with her mother and little brother. But scary in other ways.

There was the noise of London – the lorries

which rattled like troop carriers, and the buses which suddenly hissed their brakes like rockets skimming overhead. And those low aeroplanes, coming into the City Airport – which still had Ugaso's mother ducking her head as if they might be carrying bombs.

And there was another sort of scary which was just as bad, in its own way. The scare of being on their own, the three of them, in the flats where they lived, as high as kites fly. The three of them without Ugaso's father, Yasin, who'd got them out of Hargeisa and on to the trail across the mountains before he went off to fight against the other clan. On their own without a word of English.

But Ugaso's father had been a teacher, and he spoke good English; and if only he were here, it would help them in this foreign land.

Ugaso came to school every day and tried like mad to understand what people were saying. But at night she cried for her father and stained her face with tears.

She dreamed one special dream – of one day going to the airport with her mother and brother, and seeing him coming through that door from where the aeroplanes land. Come to make them all together again. After that, everything would be a million times better.

Ugaso's teacher, who was a kind man, clapped his hands. Ugaso sat up straight, on the instant. He clapped his hands again, and one by one the others stopped what they were doing and started to listen to him.

'Xx'xx xxxxx xx xxx xxxxxxx,' he said. It meant nothing to Ugaso. He looked especially at her and opened and closed his hands like the opening and closing of a book. 'Xxxxx,' he said.

Ugaso thought she understood. It was something about books. But it wasn't going to happen in here, because all the others were scraping back chairs, getting books out of their trays and lining up with them at the classroom door. The class was going somewhere else; probably to the library.

Ugaso looked in her own tray for a book and took out the only one she had, a Maths book.

'Xxx xxxx!' Patti on her table was shaking her head, as if Ugaso were a bit stupid. She took the book off her and put it back in the tray. 'Xxxx xx.' She did a 'come on' with a finger, and a jerk with her head. 'Xxxx xx.'

That had to mean, 'Come with me', or something like it.

Ugaso went, and put herself on the end of the line of children at the door, all of them holding on to books, except her.

The library was on the floor underneath. This school had three floors, with lots of little landings and rooms in between. Not a bit like Ugaso's old school, in Hargeisa. Her Islamic school back home had been long and low and painted in a smooth white wash – until the looters had come and the flames had blackened it.

This London school had lots of small bricks in patterns, and from the yard outside it seemed to go up high enough to scrape the bellies of the aeroplanes as they went over. So much of London went *up* instead of *along*.

Ugaso's class led on down the stairs, round and round – everyone talking, some jumping, till suddenly the teacher stopped the lot of them.

'Xxx xxxxx! Xx xx xxx'x xx xxxxx xx'xx xx xxxx xxx xxx'x xxxxxx xxx books.'

Ugaso smiled. That last word she recognised. *Books*.

'Books,' she said to Patti.

'Xxxx xxxxx xxxxxxxx!' the teacher said crossly, pointing back up the stairs. He wagged his finger at Ugaso and frowned. Ugaso knew what that meant, no problem. That look needed no words, in any language. He wasn't pleased.

Her face went long and her mouth went small. It was the first time he'd been upset with her.

They went into the library. It wasn't a lot different to the library in her old school in Hargeisa, except it was bigger. And this one didn't just have books. All down one side of the room there was a line of tables with computers on them.

The teacher sat at a teachers' table and marked off the books the others were giving back. The children went off to choose new ones, in between laughing and pulling faces through the shelves. Till he clapped his hands again, loud as a gunshot, and shouted at them, like a warrior.

'Xxx, xxx, xxx xxx!' He pointed at three children. 'Xxxx xxxxx, xx xxx xxxx!' The three went and stood by the door, hanging their heads – but smiling at the floor.

Ugaso wasn't smiling, though. No way! She had shivered, and all at once she was crying. It had been just like that day her father had told her about; when the teachers had been lined up in the school yard like bad children, and 'You, you and you!' the government soldiers had shouted. And Ugaso always thanked Allah that her father hadn't been one of them. Because the chosen three had been marched off round a corner, and a gun had fired, three times.

'X'x xxxxx, Ugaso.' The teacher had come over and was offering a tissue from the box on the table. He was bending to her, putting his hands together as if in prayer, asking her to forgive him. 'Come with me. Come on.'

She went with him. Even through her tears she understood those words. But she knew she couldn't *start* to make him understand what had made her cry. Perhaps one day she would, when her English was better, if she could ever bear to tell him. If she could bear to think about how much danger her father was still in, fighting those other clansmen – shooting a gun, and having guns shooting against him.

The teacher took her to a computer and loaded a disc. 'Patti, come xxx xxxx.'

Patti came over. She was smiling, one of those double sorts of smiles; both at being picked to help; and a little bit of showing-off for knowing how to work this thing.

Ugaso looked at Patti, who was staring at the screen without blinking; not saying anything with her mouth, but her face saying she was going to surprise Ugaso with something. It had the cool look of Ugaso's father doing one of his magic tricks.

And she suddenly turned to Ugaso as if she had invented rice and maize. Ugaso looked at the computer screen.

In front of her was a page of unreadable writing; but what grabbed her eye was a picture. A picture she knew.

A picture from Somalia! There was no mistaking it – a scene of acacia trees by a stream, and a woman with a pot on her head coming to get water, and in the background, camels. Overhead, the sky was clear and blue, with no shell-burst clouds or rocket trails. Ugaso could almost hear the peaceful bleating of sheep.

Her mouth opened, and a Somali sound clicked in her throat. Her eyes closed in a 'thank you', and she gave a small smile of great pleasure.

This picture was of the northern lands. This was what it was like, outside the town, where the animals were grazed.

Ugaso sat, and she stared. Patti reached for the mouse to change the screen, but Ugaso stopped her with a word she found she knew.

'No.'

The picture stayed; and although it didn't move, when Ugaso half-closed her eyes, it seemed to come to life; she could almost see her father walking down through those acacia trees from where the camels were, swinging a bucket to get water of his own – and laughing the way he did when things were the way they ought to be.

'Xx xx xxxx?' The teacher had come up behind her and was looking at the picture, too. He was asking her a question, Ugaso could tell that. He squinted at the text and ran his finger along the line of acacia trees on the screen.

'Acacia xxxxx,' he said.

'Acacia,' said Ugaso; but more like 'a-cass-ia'.

'Trees,' he said.

'Treeees.' Now she knew that word, too.

And her smile told him she had what she wanted. A picture of home.

That night, in the high flat, Ugaso had a new dream. It wasn't of her father at the airport, but of her father in the computer picture, still coming down through the acacia trees. But before he ever got close enough for her to hear his laugh or to touch his hand, he disappeared.

Ugaso woke, and turned her pillow to the dry side; and, without waking her mother, she went to the bedroom window.

It was always the same in London; day or night it was bright. Looking out she could see the river Thames and the tall buildings alongside it. The city. Their new home, because there was no going back to Somalia until all the clan fighting had stopped. And yet not their true home.

It was a week before Library Time again; a week in which Ugaso learned lots of new words in

English. Now she could say 'me' and 'you' and 'please' and 'ta' and 'pillock'. And, in one of the little rooms on a turn of the staircase, she had special lessons in English from Mrs Hussein, who came in just for her.

But while the muscles which make words worked all right, the muscles which make smiles were never used.

Until Library Time. When they went to change books again – Ugaso had had a picture book without words – she went direct to a computer and sat down.

'Xx, I know xxxx you like.' Mr Cooper, the teacher – now she could say his name – came over to the machine. 'Patti?' And Patti came, too. But this time Patti didn't do her magic trick, but helped Ugaso to load the disc herself, and to use the mouse to call up the page she wanted.

The page about Somalia; and the picture of home, of the acacia trees and the stream.

Once more, Patti and the rest of the world disappeared for Ugaso; the sounds of the children in the library were stilled and the movements about her frozen. It was as if she were *inside* the picture, with the woman and the water pot, and the

camels, and the stream, hearing the sheep and listening hard in case she might be mistaken and one of them was the sound of her father laughing.

And tears ran down to salt her smile.

When she looked round to see if the others had seen the tears, they'd all gone! The library was empty, with just the hum of the computer for company. Mr Cooper had led them out, and left her to enjoy her picture of home. And she stayed there until she heard the sounds of the others out at play, when she went to catch up with them.

That night, she told her mother about the computer picture. Her mother was getting the meal, and either she didn't want to make much of it, or she was too busy.

'That was then,' her mother said. 'This is now.'

Which made Ugaso go further. 'I sometimes dream that Dad is in the picture,' she told her.

'That is stupid! Dad *was*. We three are what there is now.' And with her pestle she pounded the rice as if it were an enemy.

It was the weekend, and, as if to poke Ugaso in the ribs with what she was trying to get her to understand, her mother spent the Saturday showing her which bus took them to the street market, and how to go to the post office to get money. And on the way home she said, 'Forget Dad' in the same matter-of-fact voice she'd used to buy the bus tickets.

Fridays became very special days for Ugaso; because in spite of what her mother said, she still couldn't think of London as her home. And going to the library meant that she could call up her special picture on the computer.

She started to learn some of the words on the screen, the way they were written. She could see the words for 'acacia' and 'tree' – while 'Somalia' looked much the same; it was almost like *Soomaaliya*.

But on one of the days, in Library Time, Dean Wilson came over and pushed her off the computer. 'What's all this xxxx?' he wanted to know. 'Pillock *trees!*'

Ugaso stared at his thin white face, screwed up in a trod-in-sheep-droppings look.

'You xxxx London!' he said. And he grabbed the mouse, and her wrist, and forced her to stand and watch while he called up a picture of a big

London clock, the one they showed on the news every night.

'Xxx Xxx,' he said, 'that's what you want!'

But most library days she was left on her own with her picture; looking into it with moony eyes – although the image of her father laughing through the acacia trees grew weaker and weaker, weaker, Friday by Friday.

One night she saw the big clock again on the news, on the old television set the social worker had got them. And she heard the man say, 'Somalia', and, although she couldn't follow all the words, she sat with her mother, both as stiff as mahogany trees, as they saw film of the fighting there: of those trucks packed with clansmen with guns, firing into the air and smiling big-eyed at the camera.

One of the tribes had won a battle; and they didn't look like the fighters on her father's side.

Ugaso didn't sleep that night; but she didn't cry either, because her eyes couldn't make any more tears. Her fear for her father had gone past all that, deep into her bones.

The next day, the minute she was back in school,

she asked to go to the library; and Mr Cooper let her. He must have seen the news as well. There was another class having Library Time, but the computer wasn't being used; so she was allowed to have it.

She called up her picture; and, sitting there, she looked at the image of her homeland until it went into a blur, and disappeared, as she closed her eyes in a sort of prayer.

That night, there was a lot of shouting and wailing round the flats, with kids rocking the cars to set off their alarms. They ran when the blue flashing light of a police-car came through – but up on the seventh floor Ugaso and her mother double-bolted the door, and pushed a table against it. Who knew where those kids might have run?

And Ugaso went cold in her bed when the thumping suddenly started on their own door.

She went under the covers, and under the pillows. So did her mother. If they ignored it, it would go away; the hooligans outside would move on to hound someone else.

But, bang, bang, bang it went. And they hadn't a telephone for calling for help.

The banging became a thumping; not knuckles now but fists. And, what was creepy, there was no calling or shouting. Just *thump, thump, thump. Come and see what's out here!* it seemed to torment.

It was like the clansmen who came in the night, with petrol and fire.

Ugaso and her mother tried to pretend it wasn't happening. But when little Ali woke and started shouting in fear, they had to do something about it. There had been a pause when they'd thought it had gone away, but then *thump, thump, thump* it had come again. These people, like Dean at school, knew how to harass.

Ugaso's mother crept from the bedroom and found a long broom. Ali was carried to the furthest corner of the kitchen, down behind a cupboard, where Ugaso picked up a long vegetable knife. And, while her mother stood back, trembling with every new thump, Ugaso crawled across the table to the little spy hole.

She squinted through, ready to see the faces of hate outside.

And saw her father standing there.

Her father! Thin, tired, beard all scrawny and grey; and lost in a big English overcoat; but her father! With those same father's eyes that never change.

'*Aabe!*' she shouted, their own word for 'Dad'.

Desperately, she and her mother pulled against each other in their fever to get the door open, fast. It thudded on Ugaso's foot, but she wouldn't feel it for a week. They dragged her father in and hugged what there was of him – till they'd done him almost as much damage as the enemy fighters had.

And, in between being kissed and fed, he told them how badly things had gone for their clan, how so many of the rest were dead and rotting in the scrub – but how lucky he'd been to get across the border into Ethiopia, to a Red Crescent camp, and on a refugee flight to Britain.

And how, since coming to Britain, he had been a week tracking them down.

'So,' he said, looking round, 'this is where we are . . .'

The next day, Ugaso didn't go to school. She couldn't, in case her father wasn't there when she went home, and it had all been a dream. She stayed with him in the flat, and when he woke up, she told him all the English she had learned – and he was pleased with her.

But she went to school on the Friday, and when it was Library Time, she asked Mr Cooper, as usual, 'Please, I use the computer?'

He nodded. 'Xx xxxxxx. Do you want xx xxxx your picture of Somalia xxxxx?'

But Ugaso shook her head. 'No,' she said. 'I want today looking at a picture of London.'

He frowned, and she smiled. A big smile.

'Where I live now,' she said.

WITH THANKS TO YASIN ELMI

Small World

Geraldine McCaughrean

Illustrated by Anthony Browne

Ranulph Orfly-Nace was a large boy whose parents, he claimed, were also big.

'Daddy is Big in electronics,' he told Bill. 'Mum is Big in fashion.' They lived in a big house, and Ranulph arrived at school in a big car.

Bill, by contrast, was a small lad who walked to school as often as not, because the family car was a little on the small side, too, given the number of brothers and sisters Bill had.

The size of Bill's family meant that they did not often get away on holiday. If they did, it was to a caravan on the South Coast, which was even smaller than the house where they lived. Ranulph, on the other hand, went abroad with his parents every school holiday. It was the one thing Bill really envied him, because Bill craved travel, like a starving man craves food.

'Tell me about Nepal,' Bill would say, when Ranulph came back to school with little white circles round his eyes where his snow goggles had kept off the Nepalese sun.

'Oh, it was neat. Real neat,' Ranulph would say, which did nothing to slake Bill's thirst for knowledge.

He would not have minded if Ranulph boasted or bragged about what he had seen. At least then Bill would have caught a glimpse of the souk, the glacier, the geyser, the Taj Mahal.

Neat did not cover it.

He went to the travel agent and helped himself to all the brochures, but they were full of photos of happy people who looked like Ranulph and Ranulph's parents, and who stood in the way of all the views, so that Bill wanted to say, 'Mind yourselves!' and give them a shove.

He had an inflatable globe, made of beachball stuff, which he stuck pins in to mark all the places he wanted to go one day. That is fine; you can do that – stick pins into a beachball – so long as you don't pull them out again. Bill's little sister pulled out all the pins, and his fantasy deflated, along with the globe, into a sad crumple.

Then Ranulph went to Venice.

Bill was small, and the library counter was high. Nothing of him showed above it but the tuft of hair which always stuck up because his mother saved money by cutting it herself. 'How do I find out about Venice?' he asked.

'Baedecker,' said the library assistant.

'Pardon?'

'Or the Blue Guide. You'll find them on Travel,' said Kirby Morris.

Kirby enjoyed work experience at the library, because he could read as many books as he liked. His nose was always buried in a book – cowboy stories mostly – so he did not notice the size of Bill, or even that a tuft of hair was addressing him.

Dismally, Bill went to the shelf marked Travel. There were lots of Blue Guides (though none of them about Venice, as far as he could tell). They were full of dense, grey text. Trying to read them was like looking down a microscope at a million spirogyra.

One of the 'real' librarians, who was replacing books on shelves from a trolley, saw the bewilderment on Bill's face. 'Can I help at all?'

'I was looking for Venice.'

'Oh, you won't find it *there*,' she said. And she grabbed him by the sleeve. He thought for a moment she was going to throw him out, but she towed him to the Oversized Art Books and pulled out a gigantic book half as big as Bill. 'Now *that's* Venice,' said Mrs Hattersley (who preferred historical romances to cowboys).

The next time Kirby looked up, he could see, among the beanbags of the children's section, a huge book with a tuft of black hair sticking up above it.

Oriole Wynn, head librarian (who was fond of Victorian novels herself) had experience of small boys and oversize art books. She made a suspicious detour specially to look over Bill's shoulder, expecting to find him looking at naked statues and oil paintings of unsuitable subjects. But the page was open at an oil-painting of the Grand Canal by Canaletto – a vast scarlet papal barge surrounded by a flotilla of smaller boats, sailing down a man-made canyon of architectural splendour. The tuft of black hair on Bill's head was quivering perceptibly. In fact, perched inside the railway train of toddler seats, he rather put Mrs Wynn in mind of a Venetian riding in a Venetian gondola.

When Ranulph returned from Venice, Bill asked him hungrily, 'Did you go to the Rialto? Did you sail down the Grand Canal? Did you see the Bridge of Sighs?'

'Size? They're all pretty small, really,' said Ranulph. 'But yeah, sure. It was okay. Went to the lido mostly.'

The scheme for the voyage came about almost by chance. After a fruitless half-hour spent looking at the spines of Blue Guides, Bill made the mistake of asking Mrs Hattersley, 'Where should I go next?' He was not sure where Ranulph's parents had taken him.

'How do you mean, dear?'

'Well, I went to Venice. It was brilliant. Where else can you recommend?'

'You *went* there? Lucky boy.'

'I mean I saw it. Didn't I? You showed me, so I saw it.'

Mrs Hattersley's pang of jealousy subsided. She began to grasp what Bill was saying, and felt a glow of pleasure at having introduced him to Venice. 'Well, how about Florence?'

'Who?' said Bill.

'No! The Wild West!' called Kirby, who only listened when he wasn't meant to.

'War graves of the Somme!' said old Mr Lane from behind *The Daily Express*. He read the newspapers every day sooner than sit at home on his own, using expensive electricity to keep warm. His bad leg had recently prevented him going to Flanders with the British Legion – it would have been his first trip abroad since the War, if he could just have gone.

'But I have plenty of books on Florence!' protested Mrs Hattersley.

'Florence who?'

'Please!' said Oriole Wynne, who was not accustomed to raised voices. 'What seems to be the problem here?'

So Bill, somewhat embarrassed, explained about wanting to see somewhere, and Oriole Wynne, in a grand gesture she already knew she might regret, said, 'Well, what manner of place do you want to go, boy? In a library, the whole world is at your feet!'

'That's what I'd really like,' said Bill with a gauche shrug. 'Really. To go round the world.'

The week before, Bill had seen film on the news of a tanker accidentally ploughing into a dockside in America, demolishing buildings, sending people running in all directions, its huge momentum carrying it through steel and concrete, until it beached itself halfway down a street. Bill's voyage was like that. To say that it made an impact would be an understatement.

Oversized Books boasted a huge photographic tribute to *Cruise Liners of the World*, so, at Oriole Wynn's suggestion, Bill embarked on an ocean voyage, touring the companionways and staterooms and bridge of Cunard's finest. He sailed west towards America, because Kirby could be very determined when he set his mind to it. Also, he had squirreled away from public sight a whole crate of books about Arizona, Cherokee Indian poetry, the true story of Billy the Kid, and one excellent book about the Calgary stampede. These he brought out and

presented to Bill with a drawling 'Have a nice day now y'awl.'

Kirby had also sorted out some country-and-western music from the Cassettes for Rent department. But the Walkman belonged to Mrs H, so she was able to slip into it, instead, an audio book of *The Grapes of Wrath*.

It made a weird sensory experience for Bill – to ride a wagon train through the Dust-Bowl America of the 1930s, while Cherokee shot blank verse at him, and William Bonney glared sullenly in black-and-white. Bill would not have liked to answer a history paper about any of the places he saw or the people he met, but then this was nothing to do with education. This was vacationing with a vengeance.

The librarians put a table for him out of the way, in the bay marked Local History, where the public rarely intruded, and on to the table went every book Crimmond Library could offer on the next country in Bill's round-the-world tour. Very early one morning, Oriole Wynn brought in a map of the world, and pinned it up, leaving a box of dressmaker's pins on the shelf above, for Bill to plot his course. None of the assistants quite knew who had put it up, so no one mentioned this unusual development. But it inspired Mrs H to bring in her collection of foreign postcards. The postman saw her sorting them into continental piles, and asked what she was doing. Next day, he turned up with his own, much larger collection.

'I do hope he is never tempted while he's working . . .' began Oriole Wynn, but thought too highly of the postman to finish this slanderous thought.

The library began to look as if a special event was in progress. Mr Lane rattled his newspaper in an aggrieved way, as if his territory had been invaded, but Mrs H noticed that he often glanced over the top of it, in the direction of the Local History alcove, with wistful, wishful eyes. The next time she took over to Bill a pile of books about the rain forests and Incas of South America, she whispered something into his ear, and nodded in the direction of the old man.

While Bill read, his hands gripped the sides of the table. He was like one of those lamps which clamps to a ledge, particularly with the wire of the Walkman snaking down the side of his neck. The intensity with which he read could be almost scary.

But when Bert Lane next flapped his newspaper, in turning over a page, he saw that the bright beam of Bill's eyes was turned on him.

'Want to come aboard?' Bill said, rather louder than he meant, because the Tucumi Indians were chanting in his ears.

Mr Lane did not need to be asked twice. And a cruise is more fun with a travelling companion. They spent hours together in the open-cast gold mines of Brazil, marvelling over the photographs of *garimpeiros*, numberless as ants, swarming up and down mountains of mud.

The two were joined on their voyage, somewhere between South America and Indonesia, by Mrs Copple, an elderly lady with a voraciously fast reading speed and pocketfuls of expanding net carrier bags for carrying all the library books she borrowed. She took to wearing a variety of hats, according to the climate of the country they were visiting. Whenever they were in the tropics, she wore one of the string bags over her hair as well: 'To keep off the bugs, you know,' she explained. 'They can be a right nuisance in the hot.'

Forty years before, Mrs Copple had been an army catering cook in Suez. She knew her way about the book shelves, but nowhere better than the Cookery section. Soon the rear alcove began to reek of curry and melon, banana fritters and coconut milk, despite the notice on the doors which stated categorically: NO FOOD OR DRINK TO BE CONSUMED IN THE LIBRARY.

Since the library staff had all taken to eating lunch aboard the Cunard *SS Crimmond Empress*, they took a very lenient line over Mrs Copple's breaking of the rules.

A storyteller who came in once a quarter to entertain the push-chair brigade in the children's corner sniffed out the *SS Crimmond Empress* and found it docked in Agra. He had a particularly strong repertoire of Hindu and Moslem stories – knew so many, in fact that the library closed half an hour late that night, because nobody noticed how time was slipping by.

The search for voyage books became a full-time preoccupation for the library staff. The fee for ordering in a book from another library outside the county had gone up to a staggering 70p per title, but the crew of the *SS Crimmond Empress* quickly guessed that Bill did not have two brass farthings. So they failed to mention to him that some of his books on Africa came from Lancashire County Library, and that some of the maps of China's provinces (and the books on kite-making) had been requested on the Internet, from libraries all over the country.

Mr Lane did get to the Somme battlefields. One evening, he and Bill and Mrs Copple sat and read aloud poems by Rupert Brook and Siegfried Sassoon, and wept unashamedly into the mugs of tea Mrs H brought them.

It seemed a sad way to end the voyage . . . so they sailed up to Norway for a Viking saga or two before turning ruefully for Southampton and the end of the summer holidays.

The September term was about to start. A special display had to be mounted in the Local History corner to celebrate *Fifty years of Evening Classes in Crimmond*. Kirby's work experience was almost over. The atmosphere in the library was distinctly subdued as Mr Lane held open the swing doors one last time for Mrs Copple, her arms full of cake tins and carrier bags.

'It was neat,' said Bill. 'I mean, I had a really

great time. You were ace. All of you.'

A silence fell of the kind which so often prevents holiday acquaintances from keeping in touch. Mrs Hattersley broke it. Poking her fingers nervously into her neatly permed hair, she said, 'Of course, I'm a time traveller myself.'

Everyone stared at her. She blushed.

'I do time travel, myself. I can recommend the Seventeenth Century, though the Eighteenth gets a bit smutty. There's always prehistory, if you'd prefer. And we *did* so enjoy the Vikings this afternoon . . . Didn't we?'

The light of understanding glimmered in four faces. They slapped their hands down in turn on the computer table, one on top of another. The cursor on the computer blinked brightly in the fading light.

'*Next time, History!*' said Bill.

'A little quieter, if you please,' murmured Oriole Wynn.

When Ranulph Orfly-Nace came back to school that autumn, he had been in Tuscany for the summer.

'How was it?' asked Bill.

'Dullsville con spaghetti,' said Ranulph, which was graphic coming from him. 'No matter. We're chilling out in the Alps come Christmas. Plenty of skiing. Cool.'

'Give my love to Hannibal,' said Bill.

'Who?'

'Old friend,' said Bill. 'On second thoughts, don't bother. I may be seeing him myself.'

Were-books

Douglas Hill

Illustrated by Chris Riddell

When Mr Fogbeam woke up in the morning with sniffles, shivers and a sore throat, he knew exactly what was wrong.

'Dear me,' he said, peering at himself in the mirror. 'I believe I'm coming down with flu.'

So, once he had got dressed and had breakfast, shivering and sniffling, he knew exactly where he had to go. First to the chemist for some medicine, then to the supermarket for soup and tea and fruit and biscuits and other things that were nice to eat when you were ill. And finally – most important of all – to the library, for an extra supply of books to keep him going till he was better.

'I'll look for a travel book or two,' he said as he washed up his breakfast dishes, 'about warm sunny faraway places. And a book of poems, which always make me feel better. And some funny books to cheer me up. And a good lot of novels – especially my favourite, magical adventure stories with wizards and elves and heroes and monsters . . .'

For as long as he could remember, Mr Fogbeam had been a reader, and a dreamer. And, because he was both those things, he had always especially liked stories with magic in them – magical places, magical people, magical powers. But of course he liked most other sorts of books, almost *any* sort of book, nearly as much.

He could still remember when he was very young, when his hunger for reading was quite new, and his white-haired old Gran took him for the first time to the library in their town. Seeing so many books all in one place, he had been sure that they must be all the books in the world. The sight had filled him with joy – and he had vowed that he would read them all . . .

But of course the library went on getting more

books, new books. So even though Mr Fogbeam had read endlessly and hungrily since then, visiting the library often and regularly, he never had managed to read all of the library's books. Which was just as well, since he would have hated to run out of things to read.

And now Mr Fogbeam himself was as old and white-haired as his Gran had been, and might have had grandchildren of his own to take to the library. But somehow he had never got round to getting married and having children to produce grandchildren. So he lived all by himself, without even a cat or a dog for company.

He did often feel lonely, living that way. But he always had things to do – working at a quiet job in an office, pottering around his quiet little house, sometimes listening to the radio or watching a bit of TV. And more than anything, when he was feeling lonely or wishing for something different or just wanting to enjoy himself, he had his reading – and his dreaming.

He dreamed while asleep, of course, as everyone does. But also, like almost everyone, he enjoyed day-dreaming. And when that happened – when he leaned back in his chair and closed his eyes and day-dreamed – he was often dreaming about the same thing that he found in his favourite reading. *Magic*.

In those day-dreams he visited magical worlds, spoke to goblins and elves, and – best of all – had his own magic powers. In his dreams he became a powerful wizard who performed mighty deeds and generally had a marvellous time.

'I could do with some magic right now,' he said to himself, putting on his coat, sniffling and shivering. 'I'd magic this flu away . . . And I'd bring books here from the library by magic, so I wouldn't have to go out in the rain.'

But then he smiled at himself, because he knew that magic only existed in dreams and stories. If he wanted any books – and medicine, and shopping – he was going to *have* to go out in the autumn drizzle.

So he wrapped up warmly, and set off. In fact he didn't have too far to walk to the town centre, so he soon got his medicine and his shopping. Then he turned, eagerly as always, into the library, where the pretty young librarian, Miss Honeywell, smiled and waved at him as she always did.

Another day he might have spent a happy hour

or two exploring the shelves or glancing through the magazines on the rack. But he was feeling more and more unwell as the flu took a stronger hold on him. He wanted to get home, into his chair by the fire, to take some of the medicine, have a hot cup of tea – and start on one of his library books.

So he chose his books as quickly as he could. He found two interesting travel books about sunny places, and a thick book full of wonderful poems. He found two humorous books as well, with such funny covers that he almost laughed out loud right there in the quiet library. And, though it was harder to choose which novels to take, he finally settled on three – every one of them about wondrous adventures in exciting magical worlds.

Strangely, as he made his choices, a few of the books almost seemed to choose themselves. As if, impossibly, they had *moved* – pushing out a little from the midst of a row of books, or falling over noisily at the end of a row. But Mr Fogbeam just shook his head as he picked them up. I'm imagining things, he thought to himself.

'Goodness, Mr Fogbeam!' said Miss Honeywell

as he arrived at her counter with his burden. 'So many books, along with your shopping! Can you manage?'

'Oh, yes, thank you,' said Mr Fogbeam. 'It's just that I think I'm getting flu, and I need to stock up – so I won't have to go out for a few days.'

'I'm sorry you're not well,' Miss Honeywell said kindly. 'You'll have to keep warm and look after yourself.'

'I'll be all right,' Mr Fogbeam said, with a sniffly smile. 'I'm always all right when I have plenty of books to read.'

So he returned home, put away his shopping and made a cup of tea. By then he was feeling even worse, more sniffly and shivery but hot and feverish as well. So he put on the fire in his bedroom instead, and took his tea and a hot-water bottle and all of his books and went to bed.

He stayed there for most of that day, feeling worse and worse as the hours went by. That night he slept restlessly, still hot and shivery from his fever, and the next day he felt so miserable that he could barely get up to make a bit of breakfast, and then a bit of lunch. By mid-afternoon, full of aches and pains and coughs and sniffles and the fever blazing through him, he felt too ill even to read. Which, for Mr Fogbeam, was very ill indeed.

So, as his room filled with autumn twilight, he lay back and closed his eyes, hoping to forget his illness in a pleasant day-dream or two. At first he drifted quietly through thoughts and dreams about the days of his youth, happy times and old friends, places he had been, books he had read.

Until at last he fell completely asleep, no longer day-dreaming but just dreaming.

At the start, his dream seemed quite ordinary – simply about himself, as he was, lying ill in bed, with all the library books piled on his bed-side table.

But suddenly, in his dream, some of the books began to *move*.

Just four of them, he saw – a travel book, a poetry book, a humorous book and a novel. In fact, as far as he could remember, those were the same four that had seemed to move ear-lier, in the library. Slowly, as his dreaming self watched, those books opened by themselves, their pages fluttering like wings, and floated up from the table.

As they floated, they seemed to quiver, and to

grow dim. And then, astoundingly, in place of the four books there were suddenly four *people*. Two men and two women, standing by Mr Fogbeam's bed, smiling.

Magic, Mr Fogbeam thought, gazing breathlessly back at them. But because it was a dream, he didn't feel at all nervous or frightened. 'Hello,' he said to the four people. 'Where did you come from?'

'From the library, of course,' said one of the men, tall and dark-skinned, who had been one of the travel books.

Mr Fogbeam nodded as if that made perfect sense. 'Are all the books in the library really people?' he asked.

'No,' said one of the women. She was grey-haired and trim in an elegant dress, and had been the book of poetry. 'Just some of us.'

'But we make a good *sum*,' said the other man, tubby and grinning, who had been a joke book.

Mr Fogbeam smiled. 'All these years I've been borrowing books,' he said, 'and I never guessed that some of them were really people.'

'No one's supposed to guess,' said the second woman, young and red-haired with a long

gown, who had been a novel. 'Unless they're ready . . .'

'Ready for what?' Mr Fogbeam asked.

The tall travel-book man leaned closer. 'Ready,' he said, 'to join us.'

Then they explained. Certain people, they said, who had spent much of their lives reading books and dreaming dreams, became able at last to change *into* books.

'You've heard of werewolves,' said the red-haired woman. 'People who can change themselves into wolves. Well, we're sort of . . . were-books.'

Such people, they went on, mostly gathered in libraries, the best places for books, where it was always warm and peaceful, and where they were well looked after. At night, when no one was around, they could become people again if they wished, while by day they rested on the shelves, dreaming, when they weren't being borrowed.

'It's so lovely,' said the poetry-book woman. 'All our toils and troubles have been left behind. While we're in our book shapes we never get hungry or tired or ill, we have each other for company so we're never lonely . . . and we have our dreams to dream by day and the other library books to read at night, so we're never bored.'

The joke-book man chuckled. 'Unless I make too many bad jokes.'

'And now you can be one of us,' said the red-haired woman.

'Really?' said Mr Fogbeam. 'What makes you think so?'

'We know so,' said the travel-book man. 'Because you've been a reader and a dreamer all your life, like us. And because, now, you're having this dream.'

'Just try,' the poetry-book woman urged. 'Think about books, and library shelves, and peace and silence . . . Think about *being* a book, on those shelves . . .'

So, in his dream, Mr Fogbeam tried. As hard as he could, he thought about books, and about being a book. And then he felt the strangest sensation, a sort of rippling and flapping. And suddenly he was a book.

Except . . . he wasn't, really. He was only the stained, bent cover of a book, looking fairly dull, about fishing. With only a few pages inside, all of them blank.

'Not much of a catch there,' laughed the joke-book man. 'Try again.'

So Mr Fogbeam tried again, struggling even harder. In a moment, he again felt the weird feeling, a shaking and fluttering. And at once he was a different book.

This one seemed a little better, with lots of pages. But it was a cheap horror-story for children, with a torn and faded paper cover, and some pages coming loose.

'You're getting the hang of it,' said the travel-book man. 'Try once more.'

So for the third time Mr Fogbeam tried, with all of his strength and will. For the third time he felt the eerie feeling, a shifting and flickering, and became a book.

But this time he was a big thick sturdy book with all of its pages – and, best of all, he was his favourite *kind* of book. A magical adventure story of heroes and monsters, elves and goblins, swords and sorceries, with a bright cover showing a white-haired, fierce-eyed old wizard, power streaming from his magic staff.

'Oh, well done!' cried the poetry-book woman. 'What a fine book you are!'

'You'll be able to turn yourself into that book from now on,' said the travel-book man, 'and join us on the library shelves!'

But Mr Fogbeam, turning back into his normal shape, sighed sadly. 'No, I can't, not really. Because this is just a dream . . .'

And as soon as he said those words, the four people by his bedside vanished – and he woke up, in a sunlit morning, all alone.

He was surprised to find that he no longer felt ill. His fever had completely left him while he slept, and so had his sniffles and his sore throat and all his other signs of flu. But still he sighed another sad sigh.

'What a magical dream that was,' he said. 'If only I *could* be a were-book. I'd like nothing better than to spend peaceful days dreaming and happy nights reading, in a library – and not being alone any more . . .'

He sighed again as he got up and went into the bathroom. And he was still thinking about the magic dream, feeling more sad and lonely than ever before, when he came back into the bedroom – and noticed something very odd.

On his bedside table, four of his library books

– the special four of his dream – had somehow *moved*.

They were lying on the other side of the table, in a separate pile. And, as he looked at them, their covers began to open, all by themselves.

Peering closer, amazed, he saw that on one page of each book a few words seemed weirdly to stand out, as if in a special little pool of light. And the words from the four books, put together, became a message.

> *not just a dream*
> *you can do it*
> *take us back*
> *and stay with us*

That afternoon, as the twilight was again starting to gather, Mr Fogbeam set off for the library, with all the books he had borrowed. He was still free of the flu, and feeling amazingly well. In fact, he thought, he had never felt quite so well – or so happy and excited – in all his life.

'Feeling better today, Mr Fogbeam?' said Miss Honeywell.

'Yes, thank you,' Mr Fogbeam said. 'Very much better indeed.'

'It's nearly closing time,' Miss Honeywell said. 'You'll have to be quick, if you want to take out some more books.'

Mr Fogbeam nodded, then turned away towards the shelves. There was no one else in the library, he saw, and Miss Honeywell had gone back into her office. No one is watching, he thought – and Miss Honeywell will just think I left without a book.

'But I'm not taking anything out,' he whispered. 'I'm putting myself in.'

He gazed around the library, at all the books waiting to be read. And many of them, he now knew, were people – were-books – waiting for him to join them, ready to be his friends, so he would never be alone again.

Smiling, he closed his eyes – and was suddenly no longer there.

But a new book could be seen on the shelf nearest to where he had been standing. A book with a bright cover, showing a white-haired old wizard with fierce eyes and power streaming from his magic staff.

Time Slide

Julia Jarman

Illustrated by Shirley Hughes

You might not believe this. I wouldn't if you told me, but I'm going to write it down anyway, everything that happened just now. Then I'll go back to the library and try to work it all out.

Before I begin, there are some things you ought to know. I'm not the imaginative sort for a start. 'Mary has no imagination.' That's what Mrs Scrogham wrote in my last report. I think it was because I wasn't enthralled when she read us *James and the Giant Peach*. I'm just not into that sort of stuff. Boys flying round in peaches, statues coming to life – and time slips, they leave me cold. I like books about *real* life.

My name's Mary Duke, by the way. I wish I was called something modern, like Jade – though there are three in my class at Cleator Moor Juniors – but everyone says Mary suits me. My mum chose a sensible name she says, and I am sensible. Mrs Scrogham says I'm *reliable*.

You should also know that Cleator Moor is the most boring place on earth. I know that because I've lived here all my life – in Trumpet Terrace, up the road from the hat factory where my mum works – and because we're doing it in history. Till today only one interesting thing ever happened in Cleator Moor. In fact, till 1841 Cleator Moor was a tiny village in the middle of a moor, with just a few sheep dotted round. Then they started mining the iron ore – and the village became a town with houses and shops and schools and a library. Now the iron's all gone.

I've got new glasses, I should say, and a new hair-style, bunches, and I'm still getting used to them both. The glasses have got red frames with sparkly bits which I can see sometimes, out of the corner of my eye. So, at first I thought it was the glasses, when I was walking to the library and things seemed a bit weird. It was getting dark and raining a bit and the street lamps were flickering and the houses in Ennerdale Road seemed, well, less solid and square than usual. So I started to tread *lightly* while walking fast as I could. I know that sounds daft, but it is nearly hollow under the streets of Cleator Moor, like a giant Malteser – similar colour come to think of it. There's a *maze* of holes under the streets where the iron mine used to be – and once, in 1954, the ground gave way and the school slid into it. Really! That's the other interesting thing I mentioned. A-*maze*-ing I call it!

Jason Ritson's grandad was there – he was a boy at the time – he said it was magic, a wish come true. His grandad didn't like school. Nor does Jason. He said they were all singing in the hall when a great crack appeared, down the middle. There were boys one side, girls the other, with a gap between them or someone might have got hurt. As it was *a cold stillness descended* his grandad said, as the crack got wider and wider, and everyone gawped. Till someone – Jason says it was his grandad – said, 'Let's get out of here!' and miraculously everyone did, just before the ground gave way and the school vanished – Now you see it! Now you don't! With a noise like thunder – in a cloud of orange dust which took *days* to settle.

So that's why I felt relieved when I reached Market Square, and saw the library looking solid and safe enough, with its fancy frill of iron railings. The railings are black with a row of golden lily-spikes along the top. There are fancy railings round everything in Cleator Moor. Anyway, it was exactly 4.15, I remember checking the time from the clock on the roof because the big double doors were closed. That was odd – there was usually one door open. Then, even odder, it stopped raining suddenly, and the words a *cold stillness* came into my head. I tried not to think about it. Instead, I read the blue plaque by the door, the one that says the artist, L.S. Lowry came to Cleator Moor for his holidays. Then it started pelting down – and while thinking that I wouldn't come to Cleator Moor for my holidays if I were a famous artist – I gave the door a push.

It opened straightaway and there, straight in front of me – where there was usually a wall covered with notices – was a tall desk. It was a tall old-fashioned desk, and at first I thought that Mrs Harrison-Bowe, the librarian, had put it there. A year or so ago, we made our school – the one that was built to replace the one that collapsed – into a Victorian school. We all dressed up in old-fashioned clothes and sat on long benches, and Mrs Scrogham sat behind a tall desk like this one. She nearly caned Jason for not knowing his seven times table! I thought Mrs Harrison-Bowe had done the same sort of thing to the library. She did know I was doing a project on it – I should have said that earlier – and that I was coming today to get some more information. Our class were all doing projects on Cleator Moor. The library was built in 1906; I knew that already.

I called out, 'Mrs Harrison-Bowe!' – half-expecting her to appear, dressed as an old-fashioned librarian. I wouldn't have put it past her. She was ace at acting, really brought books to life by reading them out loud with all the right voices. That's how she got me into reading. Sometimes she even got dressed-up, in costumes she borrowed from the publishers.

I wished I could stop feeling nervous though. It was *so* quiet – that was the trouble – like those weird moments in class when everyone stops talking at the same time. I couldn't help glancing at the floor, but there weren't any cracks, well, only the zig-zag pattern of the wooden tiles. But that was another change. The carpet had gone – and so had a lot of the books, all the colourful ones in the children's section. In fact, there was no sign of the children's library at all – no bright book boxes, no posters on the walls, or teddies. Mrs Harrison-Bowe loves teddies, and Paddington and Pooh usually sat on the window-sill, but there were no toys at all. There was no play-bus, either. It was usually full of little kids at this time of day.

Where had she put everything?

Where *was* she?

It was hard to see properly. Even the lights were different, dim and flickery, and as I went to look for her my footsteps seemed to echo, reminding me of all those tunnels beneath the floor. To take my mind off them, I tried to read the titles of some of the books, but I had to stand on tip-toe to read the ones on the top row – a set of Charles Dickens books in dull blue covers. These shelves were tall and dark. Further down I found a lot of Sherlock

Holmes stories by Arthur Conan Doyle, but even they looked boring in matching grey covers. Why did they all look the same?

'Mrs Harrison-Bowe!' I had loads of questions to ask her. Where was she?

'Sss..ilence in the library!'

I laughed. Mrs Harrison-Bowe sometimes *sang* in the library!

'Sss..ilence!'

I spun round. It was weird being watched by someone I couldn't see.

'Mrs H . . .'

'Sss..ilence!'

Then I saw her, behind the tall desk, and I giggled because a *witch* glared down at me. Stony witch eyes, bony witch nose with a pimple on the end, long black clothes. And she had a wig on, she must have. She could never have done her hair like that – in snake-like coils, one over each ear.

When she spoke the pimple wobbled.

'What's it made of?' I think I pointed.

And she swooped like a huge spluttering bat.

Unfortunately it took me several seconds to realise that the splutter wasn't laughter but real rage.

95

Seconds in which she grabbed one of my bunches. 'Bbb..ut . . .'

Staggering and sliding, I tried to keep up with my hair, as she dragged me across the wooden floor to the little room next to the children's library.

'Himpident brat! What do you think you're doing in here? I'll get Constable Bull to you I will. He'll clip you round your ear!'

Wrenching open the door she hurled me inside and I heard the key crunch in the lock.

It was dark in the cupboard. In the darkness I thought hard. Mrs Harrison-Bowe was brilliant at acting. Mrs Harrison-Bowe would do anything to bring books to life, even dry old history books. But . . .

I listened.

'This is Miss Clack here, from Cleator Moor library. Get me Constable Bull.'

But could Mrs Harrison-Bowe move walls? Course not, nor could she put up new ones.

My first thought had been right. I knew as soon as I walked in – walked *through* the doorway where the wall with the notices on it was now.

Was? Is? Now? Then? I still don't know what words to use.

I found the keyhole and peered through it – into the library, where flickering gas lamps cast a bluish light. I saw the librarian holding an old-fashioned telephone to her snake-ear.

'This is Miss Clack here, from Cleator Moor library. Constable Bull? I have a himpident brat in here.'

A man walked in, took off his flat cap, and shook his orange hair. He carried a lamp and a box. A miner's lamp. A bait box. Bait was dinner. I'd seen old brown photos showing such things.

'It be slatherly oot, Miss Clack,' he said.

She ignored him.

'Ay, it be pelting doon,' he said to no-one in particular.

Replacing the phone, she glanced down at him.

'Hands, Mr Duke!'

To my amazement he held them up for inspection.

'Ah've come for *Mary Barton*, by Mrs Gaskell,' he said, when she'd nodded for him to lower his hands. 'Ah' asked for it last Wednesday.'

I could see her bony fingers riffling through the

tickets. 'But you've not brought back your last book, Mr Duke,' she said at last.

Mr Duke!

'I did tha' Miss Clack . . .'

'You did *not*, Mr Duke!' She glared down at him. 'The ticket's still here for it.'

'Then you must've forgot to tek it oot, Miss Clack.'

'I did *not*, Mr Duke!'

Then a fat, red-faced policeman stomped in, in high black boots. He took off his peaked hat and his bald head steamed.

'Where be the himpident brat then, Miss Clack?'

'In the cupboard, Constable Bull. Here's the key.'

As he approached, he clapped his white-gloved hands together. Clink. Clink.

Frozen with fear, I couldn't move from the keyhole. I just watched those clinking white hands coming closer and closer, till they covered the hole and it went dark again.

Terrified, I heard the key clunk into the lock.

Heard it grind.

Felt the door opening, knocking me backwards.

Staggering, I felt my head hit something hard, then, huddled in the corner of the cupboard, I waited for the policeman to find me. What would he do? I was gibbering, I know I was.

Then a light came on – a bright white electric light – and there was a postman! Not a *police*man, but a *post*man! Postman Pat to be precise!

He took off his head and there was Mrs Harrison-Bowe's much prettier one.

'Mary!' she saw me and jumped. 'What *are* you doing in here?'

She helped me to my feet and I looked out of the door past her – at the red and yellow play-bus on the blue carpet, at the dragon poster on the wall, at Paddington Bear and Winnie the Pooh sitting on the window-sill, at the shelves of glossy picture books and the carousel of paperbacks near the story-tapes.

Mrs Harrison-Bowe was propping open the door with a chair.

'I'd have warned you about that door locking, but I never thought you'd come into the office on your own, Mary. Couldn't you wait to look at these things I've got for you?'

She picked up a huge old book. 'What do you think this is?'

'The library ledger which shows who took books out?' I said.

'Right!' she said.

I took it from her eagerly. 'Now if I was the very first librarian of this library I wouldn't have let you have that . . .'

'. . . till you'd inspected my hands,' I said, 'to see if they were clean enough.'

'Yes,' she said. 'How did you know that?'

She went on, 'In fact, I wouldn't have let you into the library at all. Children weren't allowed in then, you know.'

I kept quiet.

'Miss Clack, the first librarian, she were a right tartar, the old folk say. She ruled this place with a rod of iron. Made grown men blench. Wouldn't let them have any book they liked, you know. She only let them have what she thought was suitable.'

I looked through the ledger. It was a bit disappointing because it didn't give the titles of the books people borrowed, or the dates they borrowed them. It only gave their names and addresses and the date they joined the library.

But there it was, my great great grandad's name.

Fred Duke, 5 Fletcher Street, Cleator Moor.
Joined 29th April 1911.

It made me feel all prickly. And when I left the library, the clock outside said 4.30, though my watch said 5.00. There. I've written down exactly what happened. Extraordinary? I call it extra-weird.

PS   Miss Senogle, who's the oldest person in Cleator Moor, says Constable Bull used to keep marbles in his glove, so when he did clip you round the ear it really hurt. I think I had a lucky escape!

How to Live Forever

Mary Hoffman

Illustrated by Jolyne Knox

It was some time before I realised we had a ghost.
First there was all the business of moving and then
the strangeness of living in a really old house. Not
that we lived in the whole house of course – we
just had the usual sort of unit – but the building
was old.

I mean *really* old. It only had four storeys for
instance and we were on the ground floor. I'd
never lived so close to the ground before, so that
was weird for a start.

But my parents have always liked old things
and they thought a 'turn of the century' house

was a kind of status symbol. It wasn't till much later that I found out it had never been intended as a house, I mean as a place to live.

I first saw the ghost outside my sleep-room window one evening as it was getting dark. He wasn't obviously a ghost, not semi-transparent, or glowing or anything. He just looked like an ordinary man, not old but not young, nothing unusual apart from the old-fashioned clothes he wore. And he had nothing on his head, so I could see his face clearly.

It was more his behaviour that was peculiar. He was carrying something under his arm – I couldn't make out what – and he came up to the window and sort of squashed his nose up against it, looking in, as if he couldn't see me. And then he vanished.

I don't mean that I turned my light on and couldn't see him any more, or that he moved quickly away. He just disappeared – there one minute and gone the next, like a wiped computer file.

I don't know why I didn't tell my parents. I suppose because I knew they wouldn't believe

me. I wasn't sure I believed myself. So I decided to wait and see if he turned up again, preferably when my parents were around.

I didn't have to wait long. I was networking on the Internet with one of my friend-groups, nattering on about moving into this old building, when all of a sudden the image of my netfriend Marcia in California dissolved and was replaced by this weird guy's face.

I froze in mid-sentence. The voice-box, instead of transmitting Marcia's cheerful tones, gave out a sound like slowed-up speech. I could see the guy's mouth moving so I knew he must have been speaking into his computer, but the reception was awful.

Eventually, I realised he was trying to ask me my name.

'Cruise,' I said, but he looked puzzled, so I asked him his.

It sounded like 'Mister Beresford'. That was weird too. People were only called 'Mister' on our History modules. I wondered if it was a first name like 'Junior' or 'Boss'.

This net-talking with a ghost wasn't getting me very far.

'What do you want?' I tried.

'Let me in,' said the slow voice. 'You must let me in.'

'No way!' I said and closed the connection.

I sat in front of the screen and found I was shaking. 'Mister Beresford' didn't look frightening in himself, but let him in? Did he think I was crazy, or something? Anyway, he *was* in, in a spooky sort of way, if he could infiltrate the Net.

The next day, someone tried to operate the door code and got it wrong. Not on the unit, but on the front door of the building. It set off the automatic alert and a security team came round, but they found nothing. Of course not. If it had been Mister Beresford, he would just have disappeared. And I was pretty sure it was him.

But if he was a ghost, why didn't he just walk through the walls? Straightaway, I wished I hadn't thought that. I kept thinking about it all day and when I went to bed, I knew I was going to have trouble sleeping and, when I *did* manage to drop off, I had awful nightmares about people materialising down the modem.

'What is it, Cruise?' asked my mother, the third

time I woke up screaming. 'Is something troubling you? Surely you're not still unsettled by the move?'

'I think I may be,' I said, still trembling. 'We've never lived in an old house before. It spooks me.'

'Oh, darling,' said my mother. 'It's just a building. How can old bricks be spooky?'

'I don't know,' I said, 'but I think we may have a ghost. I've seen things I can't understand.'

My mother frowned. 'What *you've* seen is too many scary videos. I'll have to check the control chip. Now settle down and go to sleep. Ghosts indeed! You'd think you were living in the twentieth century.'

So I thought I'd have to cope with this on my own. I waited till I heard Mum go back into her room and then got up. I couldn't get to sleep until I had sorted something out; I was a wreck. I decided to contact Mister Beresford myself.

As soon as I logged in, I was deluged with waiting messages. I hadn't switched the computer on at all, except to go to school, since the day the ghost had contacted me on the Internet.

'Cruise,' said the computer, 'you have two hundred and five messages. Do you want to see the list?'

'Yes,' I said and ran down the names. One was Mr B. 'Mr' – that was how they used to write Mister in the olden days.

'Open message sixty-two,' I said, 'no visuals.' I couldn't cope with seeing Mr B's face.

Dear Bruce, the message read, I hope that is your name. I couldn't quite catch it. Please don't be afraid. I mean you no harm. But I need to come into the building on the corner of First Avenue and Millennium Street. You are in there, aren't you? There's something I need to do there, so that I can R.I.P. Please reply.

'Computer,' I said, 'what does R.I.P. mean?'

'It is an abbreviation of a Latin phrase, Requiescat in Pace. It means Rest in Peace. It was commonly put on stone memorials in the days when dead people were buried in the earth, before cryogenics was common practice.'

Latin? Surely Mister Beresford was not *that* old? But R.I.P.-ing sounded a convincingly ghosty sort of thing for him to want to do.

Before I could change my mind, I sent him a quick message saying 'Be at the front door at midnight.'

If I was going to meet a ghost, I was going to do it properly.

At midnight, when my parents were asleep, I crept out of the unit, wedging the door open with my father's outdoor helmet. I had mine on as I opened the front door. Mr Beresford was already there. We both jumped.

'Hello, Bruce,' he said.

'Hello, Mr Beresford,' I said. 'My name's Cruise, actually, not Bruce.'

'Why have you got that thing on your head?' he asked.

'Because of adjusting from a controlled atmosphere,' I answered. The fact that he didn't know and wasn't wearing a helmet himself, was enough to confirm that he came from an earlier time. That and the fact that he was wearing the old-fashioned suit and tie he'd had on the first time I saw him.

He was still carrying something, and now I could see it was a book; another sign that he came from the past. I had seen books before, of course, on History modules and in the Virtual Museum. I'd even held one there and riffled through the paper pages. It was weird. But not as weird as Mister Beresford.

I swallowed hard. 'Are you a ghost?'

I just came out with it and it sounded terribly rude, like asking someone if they had an embarrassing illness, but I couldn't help it. Mr Beresford looked puzzled.

'I suppose I am,' he said thoughtfully. 'Not that I think of it like that. I suppose I just think "unfinished business".'

He looked terribly sad, saying that and clutching his old-fashioned book. Suddenly I didn't feel scared any more.

'Do you want to come into the unit?' I asked. I'd have to turn the bioscan off and my parents would have a fit if they knew I'd invited an unauthorised and unscreened person in, but perhaps a dead person wouldn't count.

Mr Beresford looked round the entrance hall. 'I want to go in that door on the right,' he said.

'That's our unit,' I said patiently. I led him in, fixed the scanner, closed the door and took my helmet off.

'Now there,' he said, nodding towards the door of my room. We went in and he looked eagerly round. Then he collapsed on the edge of my sleep-section and burst into tears.

I'd never seen a grown-up cry before, and it didn't make a bit of difference that this was a dead one. But I didn't know how to comfort him. I was terrified that if I tried to pat his shoulder, my hand might go through it. But I was really worried that if he carried on sobbing that loudly, one of my parents would come in, thinking I was having another nightmare.

'There, there,' I said awkwardly. 'Don't cry. I'll help you R.I.P. What is it you have to do?'

But that just made him cry louder.

'I can't do it,' he said. 'It's all gone. Counter, computer, shelves. Nothing there any more.'

'There's the computer,' I said. 'And I have got shelves. Look!'

I didn't have the faintest idea what he meant.

'You don't understand,' he moaned, shaking his old book. 'I must give this back.'

'Who to?' I asked. 'Isn't it yours?'

The ghost wrung his hands in despair. 'No, no, I – I stole it.'

So now he was a thief as well as a ghost.

'It's a library book,' he explained. 'I took it out

in January 2000 and I should have taken it back three weeks later. But I didn't.'

'Why not?'

'I died.'

Well, that seemed a pretty good reason to me for not returning a book, but I had the feeling Mr Beresford was not telling the whole truth. He had a shifty expression in his eyes.

'I don't see why that would stop you from R.I.P-ing,' I said.

'You wouldn't,' he said. 'I don't suppose you even *have* libraries any more.'

'Yes, of course we do,' I said. 'Only they aren't in special buildings. The things come to us instead of us going to them, through the computer. You can't forget to return something because you never take it away. I mean you can read anything you like but it's still there in the computer library and anyone else can read it at the same time.'

The ghost looked mournful. 'Not like my day. You mean you don't have books like these any more?' He held it out to me.

'Not with pages like that,' I said, putting out my hand to take it. My hand closed on nothingness. It was a ghost book.

We both looked rather uncomfortable. 'Why did you want to bring it here?' I asked to break the tension, as he picked up the dropped book.

'This was the library, of course,' said the ghost. 'The brand-new library built in 1999, to celebrate the Millennium.'

It gave me an odd shiver to think of this building, so valued by my parents for being ancient, as being brand-new.

'The issue counter was right here,' said Mr Beresford, looking at my study-carrel.

Something about the way he was clutching the book made me suspicious.

'What book is it?' I asked.

He held it out again, this time with the title facing me. It was *How to Live Forever: the Science of Cryogenics*.

'Did you really die before you could give it back?' I asked.

The ghost shook his head miserably.

'No. I just hung on to it. I was so fascinated that at first I just didn't notice it was overdue. Then I just didn't want to give it back. And there was the fine.'

'Fine?'

'Yes, at the rates they were charging back at the beginning of this century, it soon reached an enormous sum. I couldn't afford to pay. And then of course I really *did* die.'

My brain was swirling. *Had* he been cryogenically frozen? I tried to remember from my Science modules when the process had become standard.

'If you don't mind my asking,' I said, 'when exactly did you die?'

'2020,' said Mr Beresford reluctantly. It took a moment for realisation to dawn.

'2020? But you said you took the book out in 2000! That means it was . . .'

'. . . twenty years overdue. Yes, I know. I told you the fine was enormous.'

Something was nagging at my brain. If the book the ghost was holding was a ghost book, what had happened to the real one?

I asked Mr Beresford and he was stunned.

'I – I – don't know! All I know is that I seem to have been wandering round in a fog for a long time with this book in my hand feeling guilty. Everything takes longer when you're dead you know, even making up your mind to do something. And as for getting where you want to be . . . Well, I don't know how long it is since I died, but it's fairly recently that I found the old library building. And now it's all different and I'll never be able to make amends.'

I tried to keep him on the subject.

'But what do you think happened to your things? Did you have a family?'

'Yes,' said the ghost, beginning to weep again, but softly this time. 'I had a lovely wife, very much younger than me and a baby girl. That's why I was so interested in this deep-freezing business. I thought I might be re-united with them later. But twenty years on, my baby girl had grown up and left home and the scientists still hadn't cracked the freezing.'

'But wouldn't your wife have found the library book?' I asked.

The ghost looked at me, first as if I was mad, and then as if I was a genius.

'That's right!' he said excitedly. 'She would have found it and taken it back! She was a very tidy woman.' His face fell. 'Then why have I still got it?'

I shrugged. It seemed a funny thing to make

such a fuss about. I thought ghosts were supposed to haunt the scenes of their old crimes, like bloody murders and so on, not moan eerily about unreturned library books. Still, I could see it mattered to him. He'd talked about 'unfinished business'. Probably the real book *had* been taken back; it was just his guilty conscience making him still have it. I turned the full force of my brain power on to his problem.

'Look,' I said. 'If you'd return a real book to a real library, where would you return a ghost book?'

'A ghost library,' said Mr Beresford promptly. 'But isn't that what this is?' he asked, looking round my room.

'Not quite,' I said. 'I'm not sure that buildings can *have* ghosts. But if they can, we've got to do something to make this one's ghost come back.'

The two of us sat on the bed and closed our eyes. Mr Beresford described in great detail how my room used to look when it had been a library, until I could see it in my mind's eye. At last, I opened my eyes . . . and I could still see it!

The lines of my sleep-section and shelves and carrel had gone all faint and blurry and through them I could see a large space with shelves full of the kind of book Mr Beresford had been holding. It was bigger than my room and one of my walls seemed to have dissolved.

The ghost stood open-mouthed looking round the deserted library. I suppose it was the middle of the night in the ghost library too. He walked over to a long bookshelf and found a gap. Carefully he slid the book, *How to Live Forever*, into the gap. There was an unearthly sigh, like a whole forest of trees rustling their leaves. Then the ghost library started to waver and my room seemed to thicken.

Just before he disappeared forever, Mr Beresford turned and waved at me. He looked blissfully happy.

'Rest in peace,' I whispered.

I do hope he does. It sounds a lot nicer than living forever.

Mozart's Banana

Gillian Cross

Illustrated by Colin West

He was called Mozart's Banana – a crazy name
for a crazy horse.

Most of the time, he was the sweetest-tempered
animal in the world. You could rub his nose and
pull his ears and he was as gentle as a kitten. But
try to get on his back, and – POWAKAZOOM! he
went mad. Bucking. Rearing. Bolting round the
field and scraping himself against every tree.

In the beginning, we all tried to tame him, of
course. Every child in the village had a go – until
Sammy Foster tore his arm on the barbed wire.
Then our mothers all marched up to see old Mrs

Clausen, who owned the horse, and Mrs Clausen said: NO MORE. If we went into the field she'd call the police.

After that, no one bothered with him. Not until Alice Brett came.

Alice Brett had never been near a horse in her life. She was a skinny little thing with wispy hair and big eyes, like a Yorkshire terrier, and she'd lived in the middle of a town until then. She looked as if she'd be scared stiff of anything bigger than a hamster, let alone a horse like Mozart's Banana.

Sammy Foster warned her about him, the way he warned all the new kids. On her first day at school, he pulled up his sleeve and waved his arm in her face.

'See that? What d'you think did that?'

He had a fantastic scar. Long and ragged and dark purple. Most kids pulled faces and edged away when they saw it, but Alice Brett hardly gave it a glance.

'Been fighting?'

'Fighting?' Sammy pushed the scar right under her nose. 'How'd anyone get *that* in a fight, Mouse-brain? Sixty nine stitches I needed.'

Alice Brett looked at him pityingly, as if he

hadn't got a clue. He went red in the face and grabbed her by the collar.

'You think that's nothing? Well, you try and ride that perishing horse, if you're so tough. I bet you ten pounds you break your neck.'

He gave her a shake and stamped off. Alice straightened her collar, as cool as a choc-ice, and that evening she was up at the Church Field, staring over the gate.

That was how it began. For weeks and weeks, she leaned on that gate, staring at Mozart's Banana as he trotted round the field. Every now and then he paused and stared back at her with his great, melting eyes. That was all. But she didn't miss a day, rain or shine.

'What are you trying to do?' Sammy said. 'Hypnotize him?'

Alice kept her mouth shut and smiled a little, quiet smile that drove Sammy mad.

Then she started coming to the library.

That annoyed Sammy, too. He was a favourite with Mrs Grant, who drove the library van. Every Thursday she gave him a special smile as she checked out his books.

'Hope you enjoy them. Let me know what you think next week.'

The library was part of Sammy's kingdom, like the school playground and the park. He was always first out of school on Thursday afternoons, and first up to the War Memorial, where the van was parked. No one dared check out a book until he'd looked at it, in case he wanted to read it.

Until Alice came.

She didn't race out of school to be there first. And she didn't scrabble about on the shelves with the rest of us. She walked up on her own, whispered something to Mrs Grant and filled in a little white card. Then she went on up the hill, to see Mozart's Banana.

That was the first week.

The second week, she came back and whispered again, and Mrs Grant felt under the counter and fetched her out a book.

'There you are,' she said. 'Hope you enjoy it.' And she smiled. Her special smile.

Sammy dived out of the van and grabbed Alice's arm as she walked off. 'What are you up to? Let's see that book.'

'It's mine,' Alice said, in her thin, clear voice. 'I ordered it. You leave go of me.'

Mrs Grant stuck her head out of the van and said, '*Sammy!*' – really shocked – and Alice pulled her arm free and ran away.

The third week, Alice had another book ordered, but this time Sammy was more cunning. He hung around until the van was gone and when Alice came back down from the Church Field he stuck out his foot and tripped her over. She hit the road with a thump and he hooked the bag out of her hand and turned it upside down.

By the time Alice got to school next day, everyone knew she was reading something called *Understand Your Horse*.

We all told her no one could understand Mozart's Banana.

'If you can understand that horse,' Sammy said, 'I can dance Swan Lake.' And he hopped round the playground on one leg.

Alice just listened politely and went off without answering.

Then she turned up at the riding school.

That was Sammy's territory too. His eldest sister worked there, and he fancied himself as an expert – though he hadn't been on a horse since he'd tried to ride Mozart's Banana. When Alice started spending Saturdays at the stables, he was furious.

'She's not paying.' He made sure everyone knew. 'They're giving her lessons because she helps with mucking out.'

He tried to make a joke of it, holding his nose when she went past and complaining about a smell in the classroom. But that didn't bother Alice. She went on quietly doing the same things. Ordering horse books from the library on Thursdays. Helping at the stables on Saturdays. And (of course) talking to Mozart's Banana every evening. Rain or shine.

But, even then, we never thought she'd try to get on his back.

She must have been planning it for weeks, ever since she heard about the Fancy Dress competition. Every year, in Book Week, we all dressed up as characters from stories, and old Mrs Clausen gave a prize for the best costume.

'Suppose *you're* coming as Black Beauty,' Sammy said to Alice.

She gave him a long, interested stare. 'Good idea. Thanks.'

She wasn't joking, either. She spent three weeks working on her horse mask. And when it was finished, she took it up to show them at the riding stables.

Sammy heard all about that, of course.

'My sister said you looked really stupid. After you'd gone, they all laughed at you.'

If Alice minded, she didn't show it. She'd got what she wanted, after all. The riding school people had let her borrow a saddle and a bridle as part of her fancy dress. On the Thursday of Book Week, she came into school wearing black leggings, a black jumper and the horse's head mask. With the bridle over one shoulder and the saddle under her arm.

Sammy thought she was going to win the competition and he was twice as nasty as usual. All morning he made snide comments and pulled her hair. Alice didn't take any notice, but, at the start of the afternoon, she went up to the teacher's desk.

'Please, Miss, I feel sick. Can I go home?'

'Oh, Alice! You'll miss the judging.'

'I don't mind that. Honest, Miss. I just—'

She looked as if she might throw up any moment.

Miss Bellamy hurried her off to the Secretary's Office to phone her parents, but there was no one in.

'You'll have to lie down in the staff room,' Miss Bellamy said. 'Have a little sleep, and maybe you'll be all right for the competition.'

'All right, Miss.'

Alice sounded as meek as usual. But when we went to fetch her, at three o'clock, she wasn't there. There was just the horse's head, on the chairs where she'd been lying. And a note: GONE HOME.

By then, all the parents were there, to see the fancy dress, and old Mrs Clausen was pulling up in her car. No one had a moment to go chasing after Alice. No one had time to wonder why she'd left the horse mask – and taken the saddle and bridle with her.

Sammy came top in the fancy dress. He always won things like that. Mrs Clausen said he was the best Long John Silver she'd ever seen, and he got a certificate and a book token for ten pounds. He went round showing everyone, and he couldn't wait for school to finish.

'I'm going to take them to the Library van! And show Mrs Grant my fancy dress!'

The moment the bell rang he charged out of school. The van was just pulling up by the War Memorial, and he threw himself into it, stuffed parrot and all.

'Look, Mrs Grant! I won!'

'Well done!' Mrs Grant gave him her special smile – the first one for weeks. 'No need to ask who *you're* meant to be. You look wonderful! Just like—'

Then she heard the sound of clattering hooves. We all heard it. Mrs Grant looked past Sammy and her face went dead white.

Mozart's Banana was galloping down the road towards us at top speed, rolling his eyes and snorting. On his back, clutching his mane, was Alice Brett.

She'd done it all by herself. Sneaked up to Church Field with the saddle and bridle. Got them on to the horse while Mrs Clausen was safely out of the way, judging the fancy dress. Held him steady while she mounted. And then—

That's when the madness always hit him. The moment he felt someone in the saddle. He took off straight away, galloping round the field, bucking and rearing.

None of us had ever lasted longer than half a minute. But Alice had stuck on all the way round the field and clung tightly while he jumped the gate. Now he was heading down the hill, completely out of control.

'Into the van!' shrieked Mrs Grant. We all jumped in and shut the door – just in time. The horse went past like a thunderbolt. If we hadn't moved, he would have charged over us.

'Alice is mad!' Sammy yelled. 'She'll be killed!'

'Don't exaggerate!' snapped Mrs Grant.

But Sammy was right and she knew it. We all knew it. Mozart's Banana didn't turn at the bend, where the road went round the recreation ground. He jumped the hedge and carried straight on, like a cannonball. Alice was still there when he landed, but she was struggling to get back into the saddle.

There were three more hedges before the railway embankment. A tunnel ran under the embankment and beyond that was the slip road to—

THE MOTORWAY!

We all saw the same picture in our minds. A

crazy horse charging under the railway, across the slip road and straight out into six lanes of traffic. With Alice on his back.

'We've got to stop him!' Sammy shouted.

'Yes, we must!' Mrs Grant jumped into the driving seat. 'Lie down, you lot! And hold on tight!'

She turned on the engine and threw the van into gear. As we screeched away, round the War Memorial and down the hill, we had a glimpse of the school. All the other children were running out to see what was going on. Teachers were shouting and parents were waving their arms about. Mrs Grant didn't waste time on any of them. She stamped on the accelerator and roared down the hill.

As she swung round the first corner, books slithered on to our heads. We were struggling free of them when she swung round the second corner, in the other direction. After that, we decided that lying down was too dangerous. We sat up and held on to the shelves, cheering the library on.

'Hurry up, Miss! You've nearly caught them!'

'He's got to jump another hedge! That'll slow him down!'

The road and the field ran side by side down the hill, for maybe half a mile. We could all see that the van was going to overtake the horse – but what could Mrs Grant do then?

As we drove under the railway bridge, she yelled over her shoulder.

'Get ready to jump out and open the bottom gate! But not till I say!'

I was still baffled, but Sammy had understood. The moment the van stopped, he wrenched the door open and threw himself out. There was a narrow strip of field on our right, between the railway and the slip road. Sammy raced across to the field gate and heaved it open. As soon as it was wide enough, Mrs Grant swung the van round and we went bumping across the field at top speed, with Sammy running behind.

The tunnel under the embankment was meant for cows and it was narrow and dark. Mrs Grant was racing to block it, before Mozart's Banana came galloping through. It ought to have worked. With any other horse, it *would* have worked. The van was in position by the time we heard the sound of hooves. We all held our breath as the noise echoed in the tunnel, waiting for the galloping to slow down. It *had* to slow down. That was the only sensible thing to do.

We should have known that Mozart's Banana was too crazy to be sensible. He didn't even break step. He just gathered himself together and—

'Oh, no!' Mrs Grant said. 'I don't believe it! He's going to jump!'

There was no time to do anything. The horse launched himself off the ground in one beautiful movement, jumping higher than any horse I've ever seen, with Alice Brett crouched low on his neck.

He couldn't do it of course. It was an impossible jump. There was an enormous thud, and a horrible scraping of metal on metal as the horse-shoes scrabbled down the side of the van. And there was a soft slithering noise across the roof.

'Stay inside!' Mrs Grant said fiercely. 'All of you!'

She pushed the door open and we all crowded into the doorway, to see what had happened. Mozart's Banana was lying on the ground, looking dazed, and there was no sign of Alice. She'd slid right across the roof and landed on the other side.

But she didn't stay there. While we were still gazing at the horse, she came marching round the front of the van, with mud on her face and her riding hat over one eye. She didn't take the least bit of notice of any of us. She marched straight up to Mozart's Banana.

'Well?' she said severely. 'Was that stupid or what?'

He looked up at her with big, dizzy eyes and she grabbed his reins and pulled. With one puzzled look, he scrambled to his feet and stood with his head hanging while she told him off.

You don't want to know what she said. If I wrote it down, no one would let you read this story. Even Sammy looked shocked when he reached us.

'*What did you say?*'

Alice just pushed the reins at him. 'Hold those.'

Then, before anyone could stop her – because no one dreamed, not for a minute, that she'd do anything so stupid – she grabbed hold of the saddle and pulled herself up.

'Alice!' Mrs Grant said. 'You can't—'

'He'll be fine now,' Alice said. 'Come on, you lot. Walk us back to the field.'

And that was how we went. The whole crowd of

133

us, in fancy dress. Long John Silver, Mary Poppins, Little Red Riding Hood and two Charlie Buckets. And, in the middle of us, Mozart's Banana, still looking dazed, walking as quietly as a seaside donkey. And Alice on his back, with mud on her nose and a great rip in the knee of her leggings.

We went right past the parents and the teachers and old Mrs Clausen, all the way up to the Church Field. Sammy opened the gate and Alice rode through and slid off the horse's back. She held out her muddy, grazed hand.

'That's ten pounds you owe me, Sammy Foster.'

Sammy swallowed hard and stared at her. Then he put his hand into his pocket and pulled out the book token he'd just won. 'This OK?'

Alice opened it, nodded and tucked it into her hat. By that time, Mrs Clausen was roaring into the field.

'You stupid girl!' she was yelling. 'That's the most dangerous thing I've ever seen.'

Alice gave her a long, sad look, as if she knew about things that were a lot more dangerous. 'I won't do it again,' she said. 'He doesn't like it. He hates being pushed around.'

Mrs Clausen stared back at her, very quiet. Then

she nodded. 'Fine. You can come into the field whenever you like.'

'Thanks,' said Alice.

And she did. She went up every evening and sat on the gate, chatting to Mozart's Banana. But she never tried to get on his back again. He might be crazy, but she wasn't.

And the next time the library van came round, Mrs Grant reached under the counter as we all walked in. 'Here you are, Sammy.'

Sammy blinked. 'I never ordered anything.'

'I think someone ordered it for you,' Mrs Grant said.

Everyone crowded round to read the title of the book and we all started to laugh. It was *Ballet for Beginners*.

'What on earth—?' Sammy said.

Alice smiled her little, quiet smile. 'Time to dance Swan Lake, Sammy Foster.'

The Horrible Holiday Treasure Hunt

Margaret Mahy

Illustrated by Quentin Blake

It was holiday time in Ditchwater.

'*We're* going camping at the beach,' boasted Allan.

'*We're* taking off for the city,' said Phoebe, dancing. 'My Mum says we'll shop till we drop. What are *you* going to do Rowan?'

She knew exactly what Rowan was going to do, but she wanted to make her say it aloud.

'Go to the library, I suppose,' said Rowan. 'I have to stay in Ditchwater, because Mum and Dad are both working.'

'*Boring*!' said Allan.

'But I *like* reading,' said Rowan quickly.

'I don't,' said Phoebe. 'Libraries are dull – dull as Ditchwater!' she added with a laugh. 'Never mind! We'll send you postcards, telling you what a great time we're having.'

(Of course if Phoebe had been a reader, she would have known that ditchwater is often the liveliest sort of water there is, full of parties and processions, though you only see them by looking through a microscope.)

Anyhow, off went all the holiday children – Phoebe and Allan of course, along with Davy, Marvin, Selina, Phoenix, Eudora, Bella and Richard while Rowan's parents worked hard, trying to pay off their mortgage. Rowan began her holidays by visiting the library where her uncle Torrance worked as Children's Librarian.

'I'd love to put on special holiday programmes,' sighed Uncle Torrance, 'but the library just doesn't have enough money for them these days. This new library manager the council has appointed is dreadfully stern about finance, and I have to work from early in the morning until late at night just to keep the library going. I used to have time to read and garden, but now my garden is such a jungle that I have lost my zinnias and I'm frightened to walk up my own path in case maddened elephants charge out of the woods. As for reading, I haven't had time to read for ages.'

He cast a longing eye at a big blue book called *The Alligator's Garden*, which had just been beautifully rebound by the library bindery. Though librarians are forbidden to read while at work, Uncle Torrance couldn't resist flipping *The Alligator's Garden* open at page one while pretending to pay attention to the computer in front of him.

But, before he could read a single word, a ferocious shadow fell across page one. A huge, hairy man with a patch over one eye, a parrot on his shoulder and a pistol in his belt was looming over them. Fortunately librarians are very brave. (Not a lot of people know this.)

'Can I help you?' Uncle Torrance asked in a kindly librarianish way.

'I do hope so – for your sake, shipmate,' snarled the hairy one. 'I am Hebhole, but you may call me "Horrible".'

'Horrible! Horrible!' shouted the parrot glee-fully. Hebhole thumped the issue desk.

'Now listen here, matey,' he cried. 'I have a problem. My old aunt, who was a pirate like me, died only this morning. "*Horrible*," she said with her dying breath (for friends and family *all* call me by my first name), "*let me whisper a secret. I was once a member of the Ditchwater Civic Library, and of course that meant getting my library books back on time which can be a problem for a pirate. I would sail secretly up the Ditchwater River, and slide slyly into the library. And then, after changing my library books, I would treat myself to a hamburger.*

"*But one day, while I was deciding between double cheese or triple beef-with-bacon, police cars came scream-ing up the main street, all pointing straight at me. I had been betrayed by my bo'sun, and I was forced to leap walls, hide under hedges, scramble through drainpipes and so on. Of course I was carrying my treasure with me (no use leaving treasure on board when your bo'sun is unreliable), and it certainly did weigh me down. So I buried that treasure under a lot of zinnias in someone's front garden, and then I hastily scrawled a treasure map in one of my library books . . . a red-covered one (though of course I am* strongly opposed to drawing in library books, and if I caught any of my crew doing such a thing, I would make them walk the plank).

"Back to my ship I ran, moving very nimbly now I had nothing to carry but library books. Horrakapotchkin! My ship had disappeared (did I mention I had a treacherous bo'sun?) and the police were waiting on the wharf. They snatched my library books, (though those books were not due back for another three weeks), and clapped me in a prison cell. Fortunately I had a file hidden in a false compartment in my wooden leg. Within seconds, I'd filed through the bars on my cell window, stolen a police boat and set off after that bo'sun. I never dared return to Ditchwater, but if anyone else had found that map in the red-covered book it would have been the main item on the television news. So somewhere on the shelves of Ditchwater Library there is an unknown library book with my treasure map in it." And here my aunt paused to suck in another dying breath . . .

'What was the title of that red-covered book?' I asked, deeply fascinated by her tale.

"That red-covered book was called . . ." she mumbled. "That book was called . . . Arrrrrrrgh!"

'Oh, we don't have that book in the library,'

Uncle Torrance interrupted, shaking his head. 'I would remember a title like that.'

'That wasn't the title, shipmate,' shouted Horrible. 'That was the great groan my aunt groaned as she gave up the ghost. Leaving her funeral arrangements to others, I hastened to join the Ditchwater library, and have been given an official Ditchwater library card with my name on it. So – bring me that book with the red cover!'

'We do have rather *a lot* of books with red covers,' said Uncle Torrance doubtfully. 'Didn't your Aunt give you any other clue?'

'If she'd lived ten seconds longer I would have known every single thing about that book,' growled Hebhole sourly. 'But she didn't, so I don't. You're the librarian! Find it quickly!'

'You must put in a request,' said Uncle Torrance. 'I'll do what I can.'

'You'd better,' hissed Hebhole. 'Make sure that book is here when I call in next week, for disappointment brings out the worst in me.'

'The worst! The worst!' shouted the parrot as Horrible Hebhole stumped away.

'A red-covered book,' Uncle Torrance sighed, looking doubtfully at the shelves.

But Rowan leaped up, glowing with excitement.

'A treasure hunt!' she cried. 'I'll find all the other kids who haven't gone away for the holidays, and we'll search every red cover in the library.'

Off she ran, but ten minutes later she was back again followed by Dora, Maurice, Handley, Marla, Lily, Kevin, Bernice, Stephanie, Max, Ginsberg, Oliver, Rosie and a whole lot of other children, all of whom had library cards and working parents. Choosing whole armfuls of books with red covers, they carried them into the Ditchwater park and began searching through them.

Postcards from Allen and Phoebe arrived at the library. It seemed there were bus strikes in the city and thunderstorms at the beach. However the left-behind holiday children were far too busy to feel sorry for absent friends. For Ditchwater was no longer dull. All around the park and the playground, up and down the footpaths, sat groups of children, surrounded by tottering towers of red-covered books, all eager to find Horrible's treasure map.

At first the search was speedy and straightforward, but almost at once difficulties arose.

For, as they searched, the children couldn't help catching a glimpse of a word here or a word there, and of course once you have read one word it is hard not to read the word that comes after it. Before you know it, you find you have read a whole line without meaning to. And once you have read a whole line it is hard not to take an interest in the line below. So many of the children found themselves actually reading the stories in the red-covered books, and becoming so interested in those stories that the books were thoroughly read inside as well as out.

A week later Horrible Hebhole came stumping back into town. His parrot looked around then screamed 'Wrong town! Wrong town!' and no wonder. Everyone in Ditchwater was having such a wonderful time. People on park benches, boys and girls at bus stops were busily searching through red-covered books, then crying 'Listen to this!' and reading one another exciting bits they had unexpectedly come across.

'You'll never find the treasure map if you waste time reading,' Hebhole heard a big brother say to his little sister as they sat searching under a tree.

'But isn't the story a sort of treasure?' asked the little sister.

'Let me see!' shouted Horrible Hebhole, leaning over the hedge and snatching the book, in case the sister (being little) had found the treasure map without quite realizing it. However there was nothing but print on the page. Hebhole sighed, and tossed the book back to her. She began reading once more . . . reading aloud too.

'. . . Hugo stood in the doorway, looking into darkness. Suddenly yellow talons swooped out of the shadows behind him and clawed at his shoulder.'

The little sister fell silent.

'Go on! Go on!' screamed Hebhole's parrot.

'Yes, go on,' shouted Hebhole. 'What happened next?' The little sister was forced to read right to the very end of the book, with the parrot shouting 'Don't stop!' whenever she paused to take a breath.

'Well, there's no treasure map in *that* book, my hearties,' said Horrible Hebhole. 'On to the next one! What's it called?'

'*The Ghastly Mystery of the Haunted Eggbeater,*' said the little sister.

'Don't stop,' cried the parrot.

'No! Don't!' agreed Hebhole, settling himself to listen to the next red-covered story.

Meanwhile Uncle Torrance actually found himself with time on his hands, for it was now Rowan who programmed the library computers to locate all books with red covers, while her Ditchwater friends jogged in and out of the library, either borrowing or returning red-cover collections. The children's library's holiday issues soared like eagles. Of course Uncle Torrance should have gone home early and struggled with his jungle. He might even have located his zinnias. But . . . 'First things first,' he muttered to himself, and he stayed in the library, reading *The Alligator's Garden*, his head filled with wild visions of dancing alligators.

'Listen!' cried Rowan suddenly. 'Stamping feet! It must be Hebhole.'

However it wasn't Hebhole, (who was sitting in the park, listening to a horror story called *'The Vampire Teddy Bear'*). It was Ignatius Croop, the library manager. He had never so much as set foot in a children's library before, and, just for a moment, he was confounded by its colour and cacophony. However he quickly recovered.

'What *is* going on here?' he cried. 'Children are taking out hundreds of red-covered books. If this goes on the council will start taking books seriously once more.'

'And why not?' asked Uncle Torrance, rapidly sitting on *The Alligator's Garden* so that Ignatius would not see that he had been reading himself.

'How can I convince the councillors to upgrade the computer system if boys and girls are borrowing books?' shouted Ignatius indignantly. 'What *is* going on?'

'We're searching for a lost treasure map which a pirate queen hid in a red-covered library book,' explained Rowan boldly.

'Treasure? Emeralds maybe? Or diamonds?' gasped Ignatius Croop. His eyes glittered with greed. 'Why, if we found pirate treasure we could probably buy a whole system of mainframe computers, and people would get their questions answered before they even knew what they were.' (And I could ask the council for a bonus, he was thinking, though he did not say this aloud.) 'Let's get this search properly organised,' he shouted. 'No more taking books out of the library! And no more *reading*,' he added.

All working parents were pleased to think that their little ones were being looked after at the library – a very reliable institution. And soon, not only children and librarians but city councillors too, found themselves picking up red-covered books from the left, flicking through the pages, then placing them in piles on the right while Ignatius Croop strode up and down shouting 'Faster! Faster!' It was amazing what you could find nestling between the pages . . . book marks and four-leafed clovers of course, along with bills, love letters, photographs, pressed flowers, dog collars, articles torn from newspapers, lost spectacles, postcards explaining that it was raining at the seaside, a slice of bacon that some vandal had used as a bookmark, half a pair of false teeth, recipes for delicious cakes, hair ribbons and so on. But no treasure maps!

'Faster! Faster!' howled Ignatius, prowling past teams of searchers. 'It *must* be there somewhere.'

'Oh, I don't know if employing a library manager was a good idea after all,' moaned the councillors. Their fingers were sore and swollen from shaking red-covered books – and all in vain.

Suddenly the library door burst open. There was

the sound of a parrot imitating a trumpet call. Then in swept that parrot, poised on the shoulder of a person with a patch and a pistol.

'No parrots in the library,' shouted Ignatius. 'If parrot mites get in the computers I will not be responsible.'

'Avast there matey!' cried Horrible Hebhole – for it was indeed he – 'What has happened to the supply of red-covered books?'

Ignatius gave a servile smile.

'We're doing our best to locate the treasure map . . .' he began.

'Horrkapotchin!' shrieked Horrible Hebhole. 'Forget the treasure map. *What has happened to my stories*?'

'The library is not here to provide stories,' Ignatius declared loftily. 'And red-covered books are not to be taken from library premises.'

'But shipmate,' said Hebhole in a sinister voice, 'I have a library card.'

By now all the searchers were listening to the argument with deep interest . . . all except Uncle Torrance who thought he might dip into *The Alligator's Garden*. If this argument proved to be a long one, he might have time to read all the next chapter. He opened his book quickly – then leaped to his feet, exclaiming in horror.

'Some fiend has scribbled on page sixty one,' he bellowed.

'Another word from you about *charging* for library services and I'll *puncture* you,' Hebhole was yelling at Ignatius Croop. But Rowan shouted louder than either of them.

'Uncle! That's not a scribble. That's a treasure map.'

Horrible Hebhole snatched up *The Alligator's Garden*. His one eye nearly leaped from his head, and even his patch flapped like a flag in a gale.

'It *is*, it *is*!' he shouted. 'Blessings on the Ditchwater children's library.'

He did not notice Ignatius Croop seizing a copy of *Webster's Dictionary*, planning to stun Hebhole and to snatch the treasure map himself. However, because of carrying piles of books around day after day, librarians are very strong. (Not a lot of people know this.) Uncle Torrance leaped in front of Hebhole, seized Ignatius, whirled him round a few times then flung him in a nor-easterly direction. Ignatius flew like a bullet into the Reference section, where he struck an old-fashioned catalogue cabinet and collapsed in a heap. Uncle Torrance turned to Hebhole, looking bewildered.

'It just cannot be,' he said. '*The Alligator's Garden* is a book with a *blue* cover.'

'But *The Alligator's Garden* had just come back from the bindery,' called Rowan excitedly. 'It must have been given a new blue cover. Anyhow we've found the map, and that's all that matters.'

'And I can see what a good thing it is to know more about a book than the colour of its cover,' said Hebhole in a particularly sincere voice for a pirate. 'And I must say that, since listening to the red-covered stories children have been reading me, I am a changed man and my parrot is a changed parrot. But first things first. Does anyone in the library have a spade?'

Imagine Uncle Torrance's astonishment when the treasure hunters, (children and councillors mixed together, all armed with spades borrowed from the Parks and Reserves Division) joined together into a great treasure-seeking gang and faithfully followed the map, street by street, to his very own jungle. Within an hour they had pulled out every weed, constructed a useful compost heap and had sorted the horse-radish from the hollyhocks. And towards the end of the day, as sunset bathed them all in a golden glow, the parrot let out a scream of triumph. Hebhole had found the lost zinnias. Carefully he began digging between them. And there it was! The treasure chest at last! Like a true pirate Hebhole fell on his knees beside it and tore it open. Diamonds, rubies and emeralds tumbled in a glittering stream among the zinnias.

'Treasure! Treasure,' shouted the parrot. Hebhole rose to his feet.

'In the beginning I was planning to keep this treasure all to myself,' he said, 'but listening to those stories has reformed me. Now I plan to donate every diamond – every emerald – to the Children's Library, provided the treasure is entirely devoted to the purchase of good books, red-covered whenever possible.'

Councillors and children cheered so loudly that, over in the library, Ignatius Croop heard their triumphant ululation. He immediately packed his cell-phone and set off for the wharf. What happened to him after that I cannot say, but Hebhole's pirate ship certainly vanished, and the Councillors, since they were forced to appoint a new library manager, quickly gave him Croop's job. As you have probably guessed, Hebhole couldn't actually read, but the parrot could, and it worked out well, for Hebhole, in return for having *The Alligator's Garden* read aloud to him in the evenings, did everything Uncle Torrance told him to.

And when Allan and Phoebe came home from their holidays and realized what they had missed out on – well, they both rushed out to join the library at once and managed to become good readers themselves, though never quite as good as Rowan and certainly never as good as Hebhole's parrot, who, after listening eagerly to many good stories rose, in due course, to the rank of city librarian.

Karate for Kids

Terence Blacker

Illustrated by Tony Ross

You're probably not going to believe this. Pretty
soon you'll be saying, Oh please. Gimme a break.
Pull the other one, guy.

So maybe I'd better just lay it on you straight,
no messing.

My name is Kick.

Better known to my readers as *Karate for Kids*.

Better known to Miss Brown, the librarian, as
SL10473 (Sports and Leisure section).

You there yet? Right. Got it? Fact is, I'm a book
– 192 pages, hardback, with a picture on the front
of some geeky guy wearing pyjamas and waving
his hands about.

Surprised, huh? There you were thinking that books just lay around the place, getting read and gathering dust, when up jumps old Kick and starts telling you about walking books and talking books and party dude books.

Books that now and then have had it up to here with being taken for granted. Books who decide to do something about it.

Right? Right.

Now shut up and listen.

Picture the scene. The Weston Street Library – a small, friendly sort of place, kind of scuffed but kind of homey. In one corner, there's the children's library. Along the back wall is the newspaper section. Near the door (some of the old-timers would like them *outside* the door) there's a rack of videos and tapes.

It's the end of the day, right? Miss Brown goes round switching off the lights. She hesitates for a moment. 'Night, guys,' she says quietly (we like that). Then she leaves, locking the door.

Silence. Darkness. Then, after about fifteen or twenty minutes, a sound.

'Psst.'

'Ssh!'

'Ssh yourself.'

'Has she gone?'

'Duh. Only about an hour ago.'

'Sheesh, what a day I've had.'

'Me too.'

Soon the place is alive with voices – loud, soft, rude, polite, every kind of accent. We move off our shelves, ruffle our pages, stretch our spines, go visit a friend, catch up on the news.

By the middle of the night, it's party time at the Weston Street Library. In one corner, the Enid Blytons will be having yet another of their picnics. Over there, the Roald Dahls will be preparing a stinkbomb. Maybe the Anne Fines and the Judy Blumes will get together to talk about relationships.

Me, I'll be hanging out with my two best buddies, Snog and Drill – chatting, rapping and generally shooting the breeze.

Let me introduce them to you. Snog's real name is *Love's Sweet Mystery*. She's about a million pages long and her cover shows a historical couple in a clinch (hence her nickname, which she hates, by the way).

Drill is big, fat, heavy and kind of dull-looking (though no one's dared tell him this to his front cover). His real name is *The Complete A-to-Z Companion to Basic Home Decorating*.

OK, so we're kind of an odd bunch, but then friends are like that, right? Sometimes you seem to have nothing in common with your buddies except the fact that you like each other.

Let me tell you what brought Snog, Drill and me together. We have this one thing in common: when we're taken out by readers, each of us has a tough time.

Take Drill. Because the guy's a bit tubby (488 pages and big with it), there always comes a moment when his reader will use him to stand on. Or to prop up a work bench. Now and then he's even been used as a hammer.

With Snog, it's different. She gets the nicely-spoken ladies. By Chapter 10 (lover boy hero has to go off to war, blahdy-blah), her pages are getting a bit tear-stained. By Chapter 18 (lover boy reported killed in the war, boo-hoo), she's getting damper all the time. By the last chapter (lover boy not really killed, all a terrible mistake, comes home, hurray-hurray, kissy-kissy, happy ever after), she's awash. I tell you, sometimes when Snog gets back to her shelf, she looks as if she's been dropped in the municipal swimming-pool.

And me? Have you any idea what it's like being *Karate for Kids*? They take you home. They read you, they study you, they learn that, before a person tries breaking a brick with their bare hands, that person should always practise on something softer. Hm, something softer, eh? You can almost hear the brain ticking (face it, I don't get the brightest readers). Then, at last, they get it.

They lay me down carefully, so that I'm like a bridge between two other books.

I brace myself.

Hiiiii-YAH!

Crunch! Right down my spine. It's not the discomfort I mind (hey, they don't call us hardbacks for nothing), it's the ingratitude. The better I've taught them, the more they hurt me. Go figure.

So it's the Kick-Snog-Drill gang, right? Now and then we josh each other about things – Drill being a bit slow, Snog whiffing of her readers' cheap perfume, or me talking in a kind of phoney

American accent (I was printed in Colchester, but my soul belongs to Colorado) – but, at the end of the day when the lights go down, we're there for each other.

And we needed to be, the day they decided to close down the Weston Street Library.

Get this. One night, it's shutting up time at the the library. Except it doesn't shut up. And Miss Brown, who's looking even paler than usual, seems kind of agitated.

Now we've seen this look before (between you and me, she's not as quiet as she looks. Sometimes when she gets telephone calls after closing time, we hear conversations that would make your pages curl). But tonight's different.

Five minutes after closing time, she gets two visitors. One is Mrs Knights, the Chief Leisure Officer from the council. The other's a nerdy little guy in a suit they call Mr Johnson.

Mrs Knights makes small talk with Miss Brown. The geek wanders around the shelves looking like he's been forced to visit a rubbish dump. My bookish instinct tells me that this guy ain't no reader.

'Monster property,' he mutters to himself now and then. 'Monster investment opportunity.'

He returns to the desk where Mrs Knights and Miss Brown are standing.

'These will make excellent one-bedroom properties,' he says. 'Complete with luxury kitchenette and full en-suite facilities. A dream home for the young single professional person.'

All round the shelves, we're pricking up our pages. Did he just say 'Dream *home*'?

'Of course, closure of the library still has to be confirmed,' says Mrs Knights. 'We've got the public meeting tomorrow.'

Johnson laughs nastily. 'Yeah, yeah. Monster publicity exercise, then we go ahead, right?'

'This library is important.' At last Miss Brown speaks up. 'It's the only one in the area. How are people going to get books and information if it's closed down?'

'Like, get in a car and drive?' says the geek.

'What about children? What about old people?' Miss Brown seems on the point of tears. 'Isn't reading a right for them too?'

'Nah, books are old-fashioned.'

Miss Brown is about to reply but the property man is sidling up to her.

'Tell you what, darling,' he murmurs. 'Maybe we can get you a place at the front of the queue for one of the flats. Do you a monster deal, babe.'

'I don't want a monster deal,' hisses Miss Brown angrily. 'I want a library.'

'I'm sure your personal views will be listened to with great interest at tomorrow's meeting.' Mrs Knights glances at her watch impatiently. 'Now, if you'll excuse me, I've got a council meeting.'

'I wonder if I could take a few moments to make some measurements.' Old monster man has taken a tape-measure out of his pocket. 'It'll only take five minutes.'

'Of course,' says the Chief Leisure Officer. 'Would you mind, Miss Brown?'

'Mind?' Our librarian is staring into space. Something catches her eye. It's me. Cool as you like, I move an inch or so down the shelf. Suddenly, a distant smile is on Miss Brown's lips. 'No, of course, I don't mind. I'll just go and lock the side-door.'

And, as she makes her way past us, we hear her mutter, 'Over to you, guys.' (Did I mention to you that Miss Brown knows about our secret lives?

Sheesh, of *course* she does. Librarians understand books – that's what they *do*.)

Little geeky Johnson is down on his knees, measuring the length of one wall, whistling to himself, when we hear the side door being locked. Moments later, we see Miss Brown pass the window outside the library. The lock on the front door turns quietly.

'Monster, monster, monster, babe.' The geek snaps his notebook shut, stands up and looks around him. 'Babe? Miss Brown?'

He walks to the side-door. As he rattles the lock unsuccessfully, one of the guys in the wildlife section – maybe *The Hodder Book of European Birds*, but I'm not sure – takes wing. Silent as an owl in flight, he floats across the room – and bangs into the light switches on the far wall.

Johnson returns to a library in darkness. 'Yeah, great joke, Miss Brown.' There's a hint of panic in his voice. 'Hit the lights, babe. I'm monster afraid of the dark.'

No reply. Bumping into shelves, swearing to himself, he edges his way to the front door. He turns the handle. Pulls the door with increasing desperation. For what seems like several minutes, he hammers on the heavy wooden door.

It's when he stops that he first becomes aware that he's not alone.

Drill makes the first move. Fact is, it's about the only move he can make but right now it works the trick big-time. He leans back on his shelf, and lets himself fall to the floor.

Bang!

'Who's that?' Johnson's voice is a squawk. He starts to blunder towards the window – then stops.

Like a marching army, the whole encyclopedia section makes its way out of Reference and ranges itself across the floor, barring his passage.

'Monster weird, man.' Johnson backs away, his eyes wide with alarm. 'Aagh, what was that?'

The Hodder Book of European Birds has taken wing again, fluttering past his face. As he turns, Snog surprises us all by scurrying across the floor, tripping him as she goes.

In the darkness, we watch Johnson crawling on his hands and knees. For some reason, I find myself thinking of all the times my readers have practised their karate chops on me. That's the thing with me – I can resist anything but temptation.

'Whack!' I swoop down and catch him a superb *haichindo* kick, knocking him flat on his face.

From the shelves all around me can be heard the other books ruffling their pages. *What* had he said? Books are *old-fashioned*? It was time Mr Johnson experienced a bit of book-learning at first hand.

Thirty minutes or so later, Johnson manages to reach the central desk and telephones the police.

By the time the cops have opened up the library, we're back on our shelves, innocent as pie.

And Johnson? They find him under a table. His suit's torn, his eyes are darting this way and that. He seems to be having trouble speaking.

'What exactly is the trouble, sir?' asks one of the policemen.

After a few seconds, he finds the words. 'M-m-m-monster books,' he whispers.

'Yes, of course, sir.' The policeman helps him to his feet. 'Books are rather monster, aren't they? I like a good read myself.'

Fast forward. The next evening, Weston Street Library is full of chairs and the chairs are full of people. I catch sight of several of Snog's whiffy ladies, maybe one or two of Drill's DIY experts. There are even some of my readers, cracking their knuckles as Mrs Knights, Johnson and Miss Brown take their places.

Mrs Knights makes a little speech. No more money, yahdy-yah, cuts in council spending, yahdy-yah, lots of other libraries in the borough, yahdy-yahdy-yah.

'But you know what they say.' She smiles brightly. 'When one door closes, another one opens.' She turns to Johnson. 'I'd like to introduce you all to the council's property consultant, Gavin Johnson. He's going to tell you all how these premises will help another important area for the borough – housing.'

Johnson gets to his feet. 'Thank you, Mrs Knights,' he says politely. He looks around him and, in that moment, there isn't a book in the room that's not thinking that we've failed – the geek is back to his own self.

'Let me put it this way,' he says. 'What does this borough need most? Monster savings in its budget and superbly designed one-bedroom flats in the brand new Library Apartment Block, or a load of mouldy old books that you can find down the road in one of the other libraries or in a bookshop?'

There are mutterings from the readers in front of him.

'The answer, of course, is books.' He sits down quickly.

For a few seconds, there's an astonished silence in the libary.

Mrs Knights is the first to react. 'I *beg* your pardon?' she says. 'You're meant to be our property consultant. What about the kitchenettes, the full en-suite facilities?'

Johnson shrugs and gives a slightly embarrassed smile. 'Last night I spent a bit of quality time with the books in the library,' he says. 'I've had a monster change of mind. To tell the truth, this place would never have made very good flats anyway.'

I've never seen Miss Brown look so happy. 'Does this mean the libary will stay open?' she asks.

Arms crossed, Mrs Knights is still staring at Johnson. 'It rather looks as if it will,' she murmurs.

Suddenly there's applause from all around the

room. Readers of all ages are smiling with relief, Miss Brown is blushing, even old Mrs Knights and Mr Johnson seem to be enjoying their rare moment of popularity as if, in their heart of hearts, they know that the right decision has been made.

And, if you listen very carefully, you might just hear some other sounds.

Like Drill riffling his big pages in approval.

Like Snog sniffing emotionally.

Like, maybe even your old pal Kick, the hardest hardback in Weston Street Library, stretching his spine in celebration. Tell the truth, I'm kind of choked up right now just thinking about it.

And, hey, why not?

Books are people too, right?

ABOUT THE LIBRARY ASSOCIATION

The Library Association is the professional body for people working in all kinds of libraries in the UK. It organises National Libraries Week to celebrate the exciting work that libraries do, and to promote their contribution to the lives of children and adults everywhere.